WHAT A MAN HAS TO DO . . .

"They'll get you," Celia said in a tight voice. "You can't fight a whole town, Cole!"

"Maybe." Cole picked up his hat.

Celia wanted to cry out, to stop him. She couldn't let him go this way, walking out to kill a man and be killed himself. But she wasn't going to stop him, she knew. There are times when a man's own code is in question, and he has to act according to his lights, foolish or suicidal or rash. And those times, if he is a man like Cole Armin, there is no way a woman can stop him. He has to do it.

Cole headed out into the street and down it, bound for the Piute Hotel and Keen Billings.

QUANTITY SALES

Most Dell books are available at special quantity discounts when purchased in bulk by corporations, organizations, and special-interest groups. Custom imprinting or excerpting can also be done to fit special needs. For details write: Dell Publishing, 666 Fifth Avenue, New York, NY 10103. Attn.: Special Sales Department.

INDIVIDUAL SALES

Are there any Dell books you want but cannot find in your local stores? If so, you can order them directly from us. You can get any Dell book in print. Simply include the book's title, author, and ISBN number if you have it, along with a check or money order (no cash can be accepted) for the full retail price plus $2.00 to cover shipping and handling. Mail to: Dell Readers Service, P.O. Box 5057, Des Plaines, IL 60017.

DEAD FREIGHT
FOR PIUTE

Luke Short

A DELL BOOK

Published by
Dell Publishing
a division of
Bantam Doubleday Dell Publishing Group, Inc.
666 Fifth Avenue
New York, New York 10103

ISBN: 0-440-20654-5

Reprinted by arrangement with the author's estate

Printed in the United States of America

Published simultaneously in Canada

July 1990

10 9 8 7 6 5 4 3 2 1

RAD

1

Cole Armin used that last fifteen minutes of daylight, because it would have to last him until morning. He used it to look at the girl in the seat opposite him and to wonder at her again.

Two days and two nights on a stage climbing from the desert country in the high reaches was a great breaker of conventions. The tedium, the jolting, the noise, the lurching, the dust and the heat could make passengers forget disparity in wealth and opinions and level them into one suffering mass of humanity. But not this girl. Two days and two nights had stiffened her already-straight back, closed her full mouth and steeled the reserve in her green eyes. Dust had powdered her maroon silk traveling dress and bonnet and had laid its gray film on her blond hair. It even sifted into her long eyelashes, making her blink with discomfort. But not once did her reserve crack, and not once had she spoken unless spoken to by Cole or the only other passenger, a mild-looking little man in puncher's dirty clothes.

Right now she was looking out the window at the first of the pines that sprang up above the canyon country, and her expression was one of utter weariness. Cole suddenly made up his mind.

He leaned forward, elbows on knees, and because the stage was going slow on the uphill pull he did not have to speak loudly.

"Look, miss. How long since you slept?"

Her attention was yanked around to him immediately, the sound of his voice seeming to surprise her.

"Why—I don't know."

"I do. You didn't sleep last night. You haven't slept today."

"I'm not sleepy."

Cole ignored that. He smiled faintly and said, "We've got an uphill haul until long after midnight. It'll be slow and easy and cool. You lie down on the seat and wrap up, and me and this other gent will put our feet up on the seat so's you won't roll off. You get some sleep."

The girl just looked at him for a moment. Now Cole knew he hadn't had a shave for two days and black beard stubble shadowed his cheeks and maybe gave him a lean and ferocious look, but he was also aware that he had an easy smile, blue and steady eyes that were amiable most of the time and an open manner that could be considered friendly.

He figured that the latter would cancel the former and that if further proof of innocence were needed he was dressed in a decent black suit whose trousers were tucked into half boots, black hat and a fresh checked-gingham shirt that he had changed into at the last stop. Barring the lack of a shave, he didn't seem to himself a person who would frighten anyone.

It didn't take long for him to see he was wrong. The girl was frightened and had been since he spoke. A kind of defiant anger was in her face as she said, "Is there any rule that says I have to sleep?"

"Why, no, not that I know of."

"There's none that I know of either. So if you don't mind I won't."

Cole stared at her a moment, feeling the color flush up into his face. He felt a quick resentment, and while still feeling it he leaned back, lifted a long leg to the seat beside the girl and said in a voice that was unmistakably Texan, "Then I don't reckon you'll mind if I put my feet up there, because I aim to sleep."

"Not at all," the girl said coldly.

"Obliged," Cole replied just as coldly.

He put both feet up on the opposite seat beside the girl, pulled his Stetson down over his forehead and closed his eyes. He opened them again presently to study the girl, who was looking out the window again. He had seen shy girls before, but this girl was not shy. She was from the East, likely a school-ma'am, from her correct speech, and she was pretty and proud—and scared. Of him. He closed his eyes to consider any number of reasons why she should be afraid of him, but before he did much considering he was asleep.

He was roused sometime later by a hand on his shoulder. It was a rough hand, so that he came awake with a rush, noting before he opened his eyes that the stage had stopped. He thumb-prodded his Stetson off his forehead and was looking into the barrel of a Colt .44 pointed at him through the window. Behind it was a masked face, and behind the mask a voice said roughly, "Just hold onto that hat with both hands and come out ajumpin'."

Cole Armin came out and very leisurely. His fellow passenger was standing off to one side, both hands above his head. The girl was standing just below the step, and in the thin chill moonlight Cole could see she was excited. Two men, one big and thick, the other of medium build, both masked, stood before them with guns drawn. A third bandit had the driver covered.

"We'll start with you," the big man said gruffly and walked over to the puncher. He flipped a gun from the puncher's shoulder holster, whirled him around with one shove of his big hand and pulled his pockets inside out. He found, besides a couple of horseshoe nails and a plug of tobacco, exactly fifty cents.

With a growl he placed his big boot in the seat of the puncher's pants and shoved, and the puncher dived into the dust and lay there.

Cole was next. When the big man was in front of him Cole said mildly, "Don't do that to me, mister. I remember things like that."

The big bandit paused as if astonished. He chuckled then and said, "Turn around."

"Hunh-unh. I've got a gun in a hip holster, and you can take that. You can take everything else, too, but I'll watch you do it."

"Tough, eh?" the bandit asked pleasantly.

"Not right now, no," Cole said softly, "but I'm apt to wind up tough."

The big bandit chuckled again and took Cole's gun. He scorned his money, which was little, and his watch, which didn't run anyway, and then raised a hand in mock salute to him. "I like 'em salty, mister. You can keep your money."

Then he moved on to the girl. He stopped in front of her and without turning around said to the second bandit, "You go put your gun in the back of that Texas hero's neck, and if he makes a move let him have it."

The big bandit waited until his companion had his gun in Cole's neck, and then he said to the girl, "Well, missy, what you got?"

"Nothing," the girl said firmly.

"Goin' to Piute?" the bandit asked pleasantly.

"Yes."

The big bandit scrubbed his chin under his black handkerchief. "Well, lady, you don't look like the kind of a gal who aims to make any money in a boom camp. You ain't that kind. So if you don't aim to make any you must have some." He put out his hand. "Lemme look in your pocketbook."

The girl hesitated, and the bandit snapped his fingers impatiently. Cole could see an anchor tattooed on the back of the man's hand. He wanted to remember that, because he was afraid for what was going to happen to this stubborn girl.

The bandit looked in the pocketbook, snorted and then handed it back. He said over his shoulder to the second bandit, "Remember what I said. And you, Texas, watch yourself."

And with that he advanced a step, put both hands around the girl's waist and then dodged back as she lashed out at him with her hand.

He chuckled again. "Money belt, eh, miss? Well, you'll have to take it off."

"It is not!" the girl said furiously.

"Take your choice," the bandit said amiably. "Either you take it off or I do."

"Watch your tongue!" Cole said sharply. "You ain't talkin' to a honky-tonk girl, you fool!"

"I never said I was. Still I aim to get the money."

"If you expect me to undress in front of you," the girl said scornfully, "then you'd better shoot!"

The big bandit was embarrassed. He shifted his feet in the dust and then said in a reasonable voice, "I'm goin' to get that money, lady. It depends on you how I git it. I don't aim to shame you, but if you won't string along with me I reckon I'll have to."

He pointed his gun off toward the side of the road. "There's bushes out there. You hustle off there and take off that money belt in private and git back here. Now git!"

The girl stood there, breathing hard, fear and irresolution in her face. The very stance of the big bandit was implacable, and she glanced over at Cole, her eyes imploring.

"I reckon you'd better do it," Cole said shortly. "That scum means what he says."

The girl turned and walked off the road into the brush. Scrub oak and pine saplings grew up to the very edge of the road, and beyond them was the black depth of pine timber. The three bandits listened closely in that long night silence, until the sound of the girl's footsteps died. The driver atop the stage spat over the side and remarked to nobody in particular, "A hell of a way to make a livin'. I'd ruther suck eggs, if you ask me."

"Nobody ast you," the big bandit said testily. "Any more talk out of you and you won't have no teeth left to suck eggs with neither."

The driver spat again and was silent. Cole studied the big man, trying to pick out something by which he could remember him. There was nothing about him except his bigness and the tattooed anchor on his left hand that was any different from anyone else.

The big man was getting impatient now. He raised his voice and bawled, "Hurry up, lady!"

There was no answer. They all listened for a brief moment, and then the bandit behind Cole said, "Why don't she answer?"

"Hey, miss!" the big man bawled.

No answer. The third bandit up by the driver said excitedly, "I bet she's run out!"

"Go look for her!" the big man ordered curtly.

One of the bandits ran behind the stage and crashed out into the brush. They could hear him thrashing around in the scrub oak, and presently the noise died.

"She ain't in this brush!" the bandit bawled. "She's went into the timber."

"Any tracks?" the big bandit called.

A match was struck; there was a moment of silence, and then a howl of rage lifted into the night. "She's runnin', and right into the timber!"

The big man started to curse. The other bandit lunged off the other side of the road, yelling, "I'll git the horses!"

The big robber rammed a gun into Cole's midriff. "Git that other gent in the stage, and make it fast!"

The puncher who had been lying in the dust didn't need an invitation. He streaked for the stage door and dived inside. Cole was just reaching for the door when the big man lifted his gun into the air and let go a wild and bloodcurdling yell, followed by four swift shots.

The stage horses, half broken at best, lunged into their collars and the driver started to curse. Cole grabbed the rear boot as it passed him and swung up, and the stage was off on a wild careening ride down the mountain road.

Cole climbed up on the top, holding onto the guardrails, and dropped into the seat beside the driver.

"Pull 'em up!" he yelled in the driver's ear.

"I got to wait for an upgrade!" the driver shouted. They came to a turn, the horses at a dead gallop, and swung around it, the wheels kicking rock fragments off into the drop of a stream bed at their right.

And then they were on a long downhill slope that hugged the shoulder of a hill. The horses had used the breather to gather strength, and now they raced down the slope with the wild abandon of a panic. The road dropped more steeply, and then the stage hit the stream ford with a heavy crash that strained every timber, and the water curtained up and drenched Cole and the driver. But the horses were on an uphill pull now, and it soon broke their gallop. The driver fought them to a standstill, locked his brake and wiped the water from his eyes.

"What do you aim to do?"

Cole swung to the ground and called up to him. "Cut out a horse for me. I got a saddle and bridle here on the road. I'm goin' back after that girl."

While the driver unhitched one of the lead horses Cole found his sacked saddle and bridle. And then the driver eared down the horse he had cut out while Cole saddled him. Cole stepped into the saddle; the driver leaped back, and the horse started to pitch.

It took a good three minutes for the bronc to spend his temper, and then Cole put him up the long slope to where the holdup had happened. A hot anger worked at him as he rode on. He had no fear of the bandits doing the girl any real harm, but they might manhandle her and, if necessary, forcibly take the money belt away from her. And the thought of it made his blood boil.

It was a good two miles uphill to the spot where the stage had stopped, and when Cole got there he found it deserted. He reckoned, and rightly, that in their haste the three of them would forget the guns they had thrown on the ground. Cole found his own, scooping it up out of the dust without dismounting, and then he put his horse into the scrub oak.

At first the trail was plain to follow, for the three of them had crashed through the brush on each other's heels. But once in the timber they had split up. There was nothing to do then but follow one of the tracks. He was certain they would lead him to the girl eventually, for there was little chance of her escaping. The deep carpet of rotting pine needles was scarred heavily by the passage of the horse, but even at best it was difficult trailing with the aid of the thin trickle of moonlight that sifted down through the timber. Occasionally Cole would stop to listen, but he had the sense of precious time being wasted, and he could not keep his blood from hammering in his ears until it was all that was audible.

The trail of this horseman sloped down the side of the ridge, following it at the same angle, and then, after perhaps ten minutes of slow riding, the direction suddenly changed and headed uphill. Cole knew that was where the rider ahead of him had got the signal that the girl was found.

The tracks doubled back now and went over the ridge, and then, in a spot of cleared rocky ground among the jack pines, Cole caught sight of the girl. She was lying face down among the boulders.

His heart almost stopped beating as he spurred his horse on. What had they done to her? He slipped out of the saddle and ran toward her, and then, a few feet from her, he caught the sounds of her sobbing.

He knelt by her and put a hand on her shoulder. "You all right?"

She looked up then at the sound of his voice, and her face was wet with tears. She didn't answer him, only put the back of her hand to her mouth and tried to choke back the sobs.

"Did they hurt you?" Cole asked swiftly, angrily.

She shook her head, and then, when she spoke, her voice was low and more bitter than Cole had ever known a woman's voice could be.

"Hurt me? I wish they had! I wish they'd killed me!" She raised her eyes to him now, and he could see the despair in them. "Are you satisfied now with what you've done?" she asked harshly.

Cole came erect then, frowning. He was a big leggy man, standing there, with the wide shoulders and careless grace of a man bred to the saddle, and his lean face was bewildered as he placed his hands on his hips.

"Am I satisfied?" he echoed hollowly. Then he smiled. "Look, miss. I ain't one of the robbers. I'm the man on the stage, remember?"

The girl sat up then, and Cole put a hand out to assist her. She ignored it, looking at him instead. "I know, you're Cole Armin.

Are you satisfied, I say? Did it all work out the way you hoped it would?"

Cole looked blankly at her and then knelt slowly, so that he faced her. "I don't know what you're talkin' about, miss. I don't think you do either. Maybe it's the shock."

"Shock!" the girl said bitterly. "It wasn't a shock. I knew it would happen, and so did you. I just hoped I could bluff it out!"

"Talk sense!" Cole snapped. He put his hands on her shoulders and shook her. "You're hysterical, I reckon."

The girl laughed then, and her laugh was almost hysterical. "You admit who you are and then try to make me believe you're innocent?"

"I'm Cole Armin. I'm hanged if I know how you knew it. Also, I'm innocent."

"And you'll claim, of course, you don't know who I am?"

"I don't. No ma'am."

They stared angrily at each other for a full moment. Finally the girl murmured, "Maybe they didn't tell you. Maybe they told you just to watch this certain girl on this certain stage."

"Who told me?"

The girl said, watching him closely, "I'm Celia Wallace."

Cole's face didn't register anything except mild puzzlement. "Is that s'posed to mean somethin' to me, outside of the pleasure in knowin' you?"

"And you're Cole Armin. You must be a relation—the son or something—of Craig Armin, in Piute."

"I am. His nephew. Why?"

"And he hasn't told you anything—you don't know anything about Ted Wallace?"

"Nothin'," Cole said, shaking his head. "I haven't seen my uncle Craig since I was four. I don't know anything about him—or about the Wallaces."

"I see," the girl said softly. There was a look of scheming in her eyes now. "And why are you going to Piute?"

"To work for him. I got fevered out down in Texas. Lost everything I had. He offered me a job."

"Doin' what?"

"Freightin', I think. Drivin' mules for ore freightin'."

The girl rose now, and Cole rose with her. She didn't say anything, and when Cole saw she wasn't going to he said, "Maybe you better tell me."

The girl turned on him. "I'll tell you!" she said in a fierce low voice. "You can take it back to him, so he'll share his laugh with those thugs of his! Craig Armin had all the ore freighting in Piute to himself once upon a time, until my brother Ted started to buck him. You'd think with twenty mines around Piute a man wouldn't mind sharing some of the hundreds of thousands of dollars' worth of freight business. But he did mind. Ted fought him every inch of the way, until he got a few wagons and some business. All he needed was money—money for more wagons and mules and men. And I was bringing him that money. It was in that money belt that your thugs took from me tonight!"

"Not my thugs," Cole corrected quietly.

"His then! He knew we could beat him if we had the money for equipment, so he had his men steal it from me!"

"How much money?"

"Ten thousand dollars!" the girl cried. Her lower lip started to tremble, and then she buried her face in her hands. "All the money from the farm in Illinois, every cent the Wallaces ever had."

Cole didn't speak for a moment. Then he said, "So that's why you were scared? You figured I'd been planted on the stage to keep an eye on you?"

"Weren't you? When I saw your name on the passenger list I was sure."

"No."

Celia Wallace's arms fell to her side. "Well, I guess it doesn't matter," she said bitterly. "Ted warned me. He said Craig Armin wouldn't stop at robbery, or opening mail, or even shooting me to keep the money from being delivered."

"He wouldn't do that, not a man," Cole said sharply.

Celia lifted her gaze to his. "I guess you have a lot to learn about this country and about people. Almost as much as I have. Well, I hope it won't cost you as much."

Cole didn't answer for a moment, and then he said, "It won't cost you anything, Miss Wallace. You'll get that money back."

"Very likely," she answered tonelessly.

"That's just a promise," Cole said quietly, meagerly. He walked up the hill to the horse and said, "You take the saddle, Miss Wallace, and I'll ride behind. We'll catch up with the stage in an hour, if he's waited for us."

2

Piute was a hell's broth of a town that left Cole stunned at first sight. Entering it, the stage driver had literally to fight and curse his way through the traffic of the big main street. It was jammed with big ore wagons on their way from the mines scattered on the mountain slopes above the town to the reduction mills down on the flats a ways below the town. The sidewalks overflowed with miners of all nationalities; and buckboards, spring wagons, carriages and saddle horses jammed the tie rails of the four long blocks of the main street. There was a carnival air here, for Piute was a boom camp on the upswing, and all the foot-loose trash and hangers-on were here from all over the West to provide it with the inevitable swindling and the drinking and rioting that gold and silver attracted.

It seemed to Cole that every other building—starting with the canvas tents on the outskirts of the town and ending with the core of big solid buildings at the main four corners—was a saloon and gambling dive, and from them all issued a din of drunken shouting and hell raising. The town was at a fever pitch, its normal late-afternoon tempo, and the long rank of false-front stores and an occasional brick building all held gaudy signs that reached out into the street to proclaim wares in glaring letters. Nobody paid any attention to the sidewalks. The road was jammed with people who walked in and out among the teams, oblivious to the perpetual cursing of the rough freighters. It was bedlam for a man used to the solitudes, and Cole felt his nerves getting raw before the stage reached the express office.

As it swung up to the boardwalk a young man yanked the door open, and Celia Wallace flew into his arms. Cole stepped down behind her, but before he had a chance to get a look at the man the swirl of the crowd was around him. He saw only a tall tow-headed, full-jawed young man in rough clothes who was listening to his sister with a grave expression on his face. And Cole knew then that Celia was telling him what had happened. Suddenly Ted Wallace's head swiveled around and his hot glance searched out the crowd. It was plain enough that he was seeking out Cole, but the crowd had come between them.

Cole sought the nearest hotel, put out five of his last ten dollars for a room, washed, ate and then hit the street again. He was in a boom town now, he remembered, where there were boom-town prices. He'd have to get work and get it soon, and that, of course, reminded him of his uncle.

He inquired where he could find the Monarch Freighting Company buildings and then set out for them in the thick swirl of people on the street. He wondered what his uncle was going to be like. Cole had been four years old the only time his uncle had visited them in Texas. When he tried to recall his looks or anything about him he couldn't. Even the half-remembered stories his mother had told him about Craig Armin were not clear. It would be like meeting a stranger who bore your own name. Not quite a stranger, he reflected; there was this incident of the stage robbery and what Celia Wallace had said of it to bother him. He didn't know what to think about that or what to expect from his uncle.

The Monarch Freighting Company was back off Piute's main street at the first side street north of the principal four corners, and it was easily identified by a high board fence that closed in its huge wagon yard. Its office, a clapboard affair with the company's name painted across its face, fronted the street beyond the big arch of the compound. Cole paused there to look into the wagon yard, almost empty of the big ore-freighting wagons now. Three sides of the compound contained sheds for the wagons and a blacksmith shop, while the rear opened into a huge feed corral that ran through onto the next block. There were fifty or so mules in it now, Cole noticed. It was a big outfit, with its own blacksmith and harness shop, and Cole guessed Craig Armin had done pretty well for himself.

Cole stepped into the office afterward. It was a big room, with doors in three walls, and a man sat at a roll-top desk near the window where he could shout orders to the teamsters. He was a dyspeptic-looking man in shirt sleeves, and he eyed Cole sourly as he entered.

"I want to see Craig Armin," Cole said, standing by the railing.

"No can do," the man said and yawned.

"Why not?"

"He ain't seein' anyone."

"He's here though?" Cole asked quietly.

"Might be. Might not."

"I'll take a look," Cole murmured. He walked over to the first door and threw it open. The clerk yelled, "Hey, get out of there!"

Cole looked into a bare and dirty room. At a rough desk, whose top was scarred by spurs, sat a burly, thick-bodied man, and he was in the act of raising a whisky bottle to his lips. He glowered at Cole as Cole asked, "You Craig Armin?"

"Get the hell out of here," the man said mildly.

Cole folded his arms and leaned against the doorjamb, a light of stubborn anger in his eyes. The clerk by this time had come out from behind the railing and was crossing the room. His pace was not fast, because Cole was a tall man and the expression on his face now was not particularly pleasant.

The clerk looked inside. "Sorry, Keen. He got the wrong office," the clerk said.

"I didn't get any office," Cole corrected. "That's what I'm after."

Keen set the bottle down on the desk, carefully corked it and came to his feet. He was dressed roughly, and he smelled strongly of the stable. His half boots were covered with stable litter, and the gun belt strapped at his waist looked worn and used. There was something about his face, the small pig eyes, the muscular jowls and the way his hands swung at his side, that warned Cole of trouble.

"You want Armin? I'm Armin," he growled, confronting Cole.

Cole regarded him coolly and then said, "Not by ten years you couldn't be."

"You ever seen him?"

"A long time ago."

"Then how do you know I ain't?" the man said.

This was a foolish conversation, Cole concluded. It didn't make sense, and he was suddenly aware that it was a stall. He was erect in the doorway now, and he felt the clerk move behind him. Then a telltale flick of the heavy man's eyes gave him away. He raised both hands toward Cole and lunged toward him, a smile already on his face. Cole ducked, at the same time kicking out behind him. His boot drove into flesh, and he heard the clerk grunt. And then Keen drove into him. Cole caught him in the midriff with his shoulder, raised abruptly, and sent him flying over his shoulder. He turned just in time to see Keen light on the sprawled clerk with a great timber-shaking thud. Keen scrambled to his feet, his face livid with surprise and anger at this crude roughhouse trick being turned against him.

"That's fun for a couple of kids," Cole sneered quietly. "You looked growed up at first sight."

Just then the other door in the side wall opened and a quiet-looking man of medium build, dressed in an expensive black suit, stepped out. He glared at the three of them with wicked, impersonal anger and then said to Keen, "What's the racket out here?"

Keen, however, was not wholly daunted by the voice of the other man. He said, his voice thick with fury, "Watch me throw that ranny out of here, chief. Open the door, Trimble."

"Stop it!" Craig Armin said harshly. He stepped out into the room. Keen subsided a little as Craig Armin came to a halt in front of Cole. He was a slight man, with neatly combed graying hair. His face was sharp, handsome, with a slight pallor which deepened the blackness of his eyes by contrast. There was a surface sleekness about him that was deceptive, for his voice when he spoke to Keen had some iron in it. He said brusquely, "What happened here?"

"I was lookin' for you," Cole drawled. "These boys thought they'd muss me up a little and throw me out." His lazy gaze shuttled to Keen. "It kicked back, I reckon."

"You told us not to disturb you," the clerk said sullenly to Armin.

"I meant it," Armin said. "What's your business with me?" he said to Cole.

"I come to take that job you offered me," Cole drawled.

Craig Armin scowled. "I haven't offered anybody a job, not that I recollect. What's your name?"

"I was wonderin' when somebody would get to that," Cole said. "It's Cole Armin."

Craig Armin's face changed immediately. It softened and lighted up with pleasure, and he smiled and put out his hand.

"Well, welcome, boy, welcome. I'm delighted to see you. But why didn't you give Trimble your name?"

"I told you," Cole drawled. "Nobody asked."

Keen Billings came forward then, a forced smile on his face. He put out his hand, said, "Sorry about that, Armin. It was just a little horseplay. Glad you're here. I'm Keen Billings."

"Forget it," Cole murmured, not very heartily, and shook hands with him.

Craig Armin led him into his office. This was a different affair from Keen Billings' office. In the first place, it was large and spacious and was located on the other side of the building from the stables. It held a rich, deep-piled red rug, the most ornate desk that Cole had ever seen and on the papered walls were a dozen framed pictures of the big mines and reduction mills in Piute.

Craig Armin offered Cole a cigar and a drink and a chair, all of which were accepted, and then he settled into the deep chair behind his desk.

"You're a tough-looking customer," Craig Armin observed, regarding him closely. "Not much like the little tyke you were the last time I saw you. Don't you ever shave?"

Cole grinned at that. "I just got off the stage. Took time out to eat, and that's about all."

Craig nodded and said shrewdly, "You don't look very prosperous."

"I got five dollars left," Cole said and shook his head. "That's cuttin' it pretty thin, comin' all the way from Texas."

Craig Armin grunted and sucked at his cigar. Cole took a good look at him then, studying his face, seeing if it would strike any familiar chord of memory. It didn't, but that wasn't surprising. Twenty-odd years can blot out a childhood memory completely. He tried again to remember what his mother had said about Uncle Craig, but again it wouldn't come. Craig Armin might as well have been a stranger—a handsome, fifty-year-old, immaculately dressed and affable stranger.

Craig said suddenly, "Well, it's lucky I still take a Texas paper, for sentiment's sake. Or I wouldn't have read where you'd lost the place. What happened?"

"Cattle fever."

Craig Armin smiled faintly. "You're a long ways from cattle now, son. You've got to learn a new business."

"I reckon I can drive mules all right," Cole murmured.

Craig Armin laughed. "Drive mules? Nonsense! You're stepping into a manager's job here, Cole. You'll need some good clothes and linen, a haircut, a shave, a new hat and new boots and you'll have to learn to smoke a good cigar."

Cole blinked. He had thought, from his uncle's letter, that he had a job as a teamster. This was news.

Craig Armin smiled at his surprise and nodded. "I've got a pretty good thing here, Cole. Looks like a glorified stable to you, I suppose, but it represents a transportation outfit that moves about eighty-five per cent of the ore in Piute. I've made money—big money—but I'm getting fed up on the business. I want to pull out and live on the Coast, and I need a man I can trust to take over the business. It's a cut-throat one."

Cole said slowly, "You mean you aim to have me run it?"

Craig Armin nodded. "As soon as you learn the ropes. It won't be hard, because I've done the spadework. When I came here there was a big freighting outfit here, the Acme. It's on its last legs now. There's another one springin' up, but we'll put them out of business in short order." He smiled faintly. "It takes a nice combination of brains and brawn, Cole. In the first place, you're over the toughest bunch of hard cases alive—the professional teamster. He respects nobody he can lick, and that's a large order. When I started this outfit I had to lick my best teamster first. I did with an ax."

He smiled grimly at the memory and went on. "In the second place, it takes brains. We're in a queer position here in Piute. The mines are high and in rugged mountains, so a railroad is out of the question. The ore isn't rich, but there's a lot of it, and it's a long distance to the reduction mills below town. Mines can't afford their own freighting outfits, because it takes so many wagons and mules. So the private freighters get the contracts to haul the ore from mines to reduction mills. We have to fight for the contracts, and just about anything goes. I can hire teamsters, men like Billings, without any brains. But what I want is a man with brains who can drive Billings." He paused and added dryly, "You didn't make a bad start."

"Thanks," Cole answered.

"Once you learn the business, Cole, I'm turning it over to you. I never knew an Armin who was a fool. The business will be yours to run. You send me fifty per cent of the profits and keep fifty per cent for yourself." He leaned forward and tapped his finger on the desk.

"There are lots of things you'll have to pick up, son—things I can teach you. There are millionaires here, Cole. The mine owners, the bankers, the market riggers, the promoters, the big lawyers, the shipping men from Frisco—they're all here, milking these mines with their stockholders' money. They're the men to know, and I know them. They're the men who give you the business. Never forget that. During the day you can work on the business—on feed contracts for two thousand mules, pasture, vet service, wagon purchase and repair, blacksmithing and freighting schedule. But at night you'll swing your business with the moneyed men. Dress well, eat well, drink well, entertain, spend money—and you'll earn more money."

Cole felt uncomfortable, but he said nothing. He was aware of the fact that he was a rough man, blunt-spoken, a hard-luck cowman who knew nothing except cattle and horses and nights under the stars and dust and sun and rain. But he supposed, with a quiet confidence, that if other men liked this life there must be something to it and that he could live it.

Craig Armin said suddenly, "How does it sound?"

"Fine," Cole said promptly. And it did, to a broke man.

There was a racket outside in the wagon yard that came dimly through the door. Craig Armin came to his feet and said, "The mine shifts change at six and so do my men. This shift is just hitching up. Come out and see a sight."

Cole followed him out a side door, across a corridor, through another door and out onto a short loading platform. They could look out into the broad and crowded wagon yard, and it was truly a sight.

In front of them was a rig all ready to go out. Ten spans of mules, their stretchers hitched to a heavy chain, were lined out in front of a huge, high-sided wagon. And behind this wagon, hitched by a short tongue, was another smaller wagon. The near mule on the wheel team, next to the wagon, was saddled, and a man was mounted on him. A single line, tied to his saddle horn, ran through rings on the hames of each near horse to the bit of the lead horse. A stick ran from the bit of this horse to its mate. The rider held in one hand the reins to the pair of mules ahead of the wheel team. Buckled to his saddle horn was a heavy leather strap that reached back to the stout brake lever of the first wagon. Cole looked at it all with interest. The teamster drove only the swing team with the

reins, the lead team with the jerk line, and as for the rest of the
spans, they were ignored. It seemed a precarious business to him,
and he was studying it when it pulled out the huge arched gate.
Another rig, identical to that one, was led into place by a cursing
hostler.

"Risky, eh?" Craig Armin grunted. "It isn't as bad as it looks
though. We only use it on a long grade and wide road. The other
wagons don't take such a big hitch. But it takes some driving
though."

Cole nodded. A big heavy-booted man came up to the hostler,
conferred with him a moment, then strode over to the near
wheeler. He put his hand up to the horn and swung into the saddle,
but in that one brief moment Cole had seen something.

There was an anchor tattooed on the big man's hand.

Cole leaped down from the loading platform and ran toward the
teams, coming up behind the wheelers. He half vaulted onto the
saddled mule, grabbed the big man's collar and then let himself fall
back. He dragged the man out of the saddle and into the dust.

The big teamster lunged up and turned around. There was recognition as well as anger in his eyes as he saw Cole.

"Well, well," Cole drawled, stepping back and surveying him.
"The big brave bandit. I figured I'd run across you."

The big man's eyes flicked to Craig Armin, who had hauled up
beside Cole.

"What's this, Juck?" Craig Armin snapped.

"Search me," the big man said carefully. "He's lookin' for a
fight."

"I'm gettin' one," Cole said. He shucked off his coat into the
dust, threw his hat after it and said to Craig Armin without looking at him, "This moose stuck up the stage I was on last night and
took ten thousand dollars from a girl passenger."

"Wait a minute!" Craig said quickly. "That can be explained and
we'll——"

"Too late," Cole said. He swung a hook deep into Juck's belly,
and when the big man folded he smashed a right into his jaw that
sent him skidding in the dust on his back.

"Wait!" Craig Armin cried.

But Juck was up. The teamsters, used to and liking fights, came
running from all directions, forming a loose circle around the three
of them. Juck rushed then, a growl in his throat, and Craig Armin

fell back, cursing softly. The drive of Juck's rush drove Cole back into the crowd, but he kept his feet, smashing down on Juck's exposed neck. He twisted then and Juck lost his balance and fell. The crowd backed up.

Cole waited until Juck was barely erect, and then he waded in, his arms pumping great slashing blows into Juck's face. He had the choice of staying away from Juck and cutting him up or never letting him get set. He chose the latter.

Juck's nose was pumping blood now, and he looked dazed. His powerful arms flailed, but he couldn't get set for a blow. Time and again, feet stomping into the hard-packed dirt, Cole drove blow after blow in his face, forcing him off balance, and when Juck raised his thick arms to guard his face Cole smashed his fist wrist-deep into his big belly.

One of Juck's blows caught Cole on the ear, and he went down. Juck was alert enough to make his rush then. Cole rolled sideways and tripped him, and they both came up at the same time, facing each other. Juck swung wildly, and Cole ducked, planting his feet. Juck swung again, and again Cole ducked, but when Juck's last blow went sizzling by Cole hit him. There was every ounce of well-balanced weight that Cole could muster behind that blow, and when it landed on Juck's shelving jaw Cole felt the shock of it past his shoulder and in his backbone.

Juck's knees buckled immediately and he fell flat on his face, lying immobile. Some good-humored cheers lifted from the men, and then Cole caught sight of Craig Armin and Keen Billings. Their faces were grave, alert, and Craig Armin walked up to him. "A good start," he said approvingly. "Come in the office now and clean up."

"Oh no," Cole said meagerly. He didn't say anything for a moment while he got his breath. "That gunnie is comin' to the sheriff's office with me."

Keen Billings quickly lifted his voice into a harsh bawl. "Back to work, every man jack of you! Step lively, boys! Break it up!"

Craig Armin waited until the men had drifted off out of earshot, and then he said in a low, impatient voice, "Don't be a damned fool, boy. What's it to you if Juck is jailed?"

"Nothin' to me," Cole said. "It's somethin' to that girl."

"What girl?"

"Celia Wallace."

Craig Armin looked steadily at Cole. "Don't be simple! That girl is the sister of your competitor, Ted Wallace. If she gets that ten thousand back they'll worry the very hell out of you!"

"So you did have her robbed?" Cole murmured softly.

Craig Armin's gaze held his for a long moment, and Craig said, "I did. What of it?"

Cole stooped over Juck and quickly drew Juck's gun and held it slack in his hand, his eyes on Keen Billings, who had been watching this.

"What of it?" Cole said gently. "Nothin'. It just happens to be robbery, that's all. I'm takin' Juck to jail. The whole story will get out then, and we'll see what of it."

"You won't do that," Craig Armin said quietly.

"Back off, Keen!" Cole said sharply. "Before you do, shuck that gun. I'm goin' to pick Juck up, and if a man makes a move to stop me I'll shoot him!"

"Wait!" Craig Armin said.

"I've waited too damn long!" Cole answered savagely. "This outfit stinks! I thought so when I first saw it. Now I'm sure of it!"

He pointed his gun at Keen Billings, and Billings flipped his gun into the dust and backed off, his eyes wary. Craig Armin's face was a study. His eyes were bright with fury, his lean face pale. He was calculating his chances, and when Cole grabbed Juck by the shirt collar and started to drag him toward the gate Craig Armin said quietly, "All right. You can stop."

"What for?" Cole said.

"What's your price? The ten thousand?"

Cole straightened up, his gun in front of him. He thought a moment, then nodded slowly. "That's it, right to the penny. Go get it, or I take Juck to the sheriff."

Without another word Craig Armin turned and went back into the office. Keen Billings stared at Cole a long moment and then smiled crookedly. "You're goin' to be awful sorry for this—awful sorry."

"Who'll make me sorry?" Cole asked.

Billings' face was dark with anger, but he controlled it. "He'll have your hide nailed on the wall in damn short order, mister. You'd better light a shuck tonight, while you still can."

Cole smiled faintly and dug Juck with his toe. "I got a hunch we'll tangle pretty quick, Billings. I'm goin' to do a better job on you."

Craig Armin came out of the office then and stalked up to them. He extended a sack to Cole.

"Have Billings count it out," Cole said.

Craig made a sign and Billings came over. He counted the money out in the dust. There was five thousand in fifty-dollar gold pieces, and the rest was in big bank notes. Craig Armin, his face impassive, watched until Billings had finished and handed the sack to Cole. Then he eyed Cole and said softly, "I'm afraid you've made a mistake, Cole. You'll live to regret it—regret it bitterly."

Cole said, "I'll live. That's one thing. And that's more than I can say for the first one of your hard cases that gets in my way, Craig. Remember that when you start feelin' salty."

He nodded and backed off toward the gate under the curious eyes of the indifferent teamsters. Billings and Craig Armin watched him go, disappearing quickly behind the high board fence.

Then Craig Armin said softly, wickedly, not even looking at Billings, "The fool. Get him, Keen. And no holds barred. Run him out of the country!"

3

Since there were over a million ounces of gold and silver taken from some twenty mines stretched along the bare shoulders of the Sierra Negras above Piute each year, it was reasonable to suppose that the mine managers would demand adequate protection from the law. They had, and they got it in the form of Sheriff Ed Linton. Aside from the mines, however, there were several thousand miners and the hangers-on of a boom camp that made up Piute. There were Mexicans, Welshmen, Irish, Germans, Poles and Swedes, and nobody could expect them to mix without trouble. Consequently the sheriff's office was a large affair, and its active work was done by three hard-working deputies.

Sheriff Linton himself was not a peace officer in the true sense of the word. He was a politician, alert to the fact that the man who administered the law in Piute to the satisfaction of a handful of millionaires was a man who might go far in Territorial politics. His office was properly a twelve-by-fourteen cubbyhole in the busiest block of the main street. In reality it was the lobby of the Cosmopolitan House, the big four-story brick hotel that loomed above the rest of the town in elegant snobbishness. In its suites, in its barroom, in its dining room or in the sumptuous offices of the reduction mills and mines Sheriff Linton could generally be found, drinking, scheming, backslapping, promising and fawning. He was well dressed, dapper and discreet. Nowhere on his well-tailored person could be found a gun or a star. He was indistinguishable from the many rich men—mine promoters, stock riggers, mine managers, mine lawyers, reduction-mill superintendents and mine supply men—who lined the elegant mahogany bar of the Cosmopolitan House this very evening.

It was quiet in the barroom, for there was no music, no girls and no crowd. The gambling—for the highest stakes in Piute—was done in an adjoining room. This barroom, with its deep leather cushions on the seats that lined the walls, was for drinking only—drinking and scheming. Men moved slowly, talked in low voices, smoked excellent cigars, drank the best liquor and devised ways to take more money from the patient Sierra Negras and their own stockholders.

Sheriff Ed Linton was at a table for four, listening politely to a very bad story being told by a newly arrived lawyer from Frisco, when a boy stopped at his shoulder.

"Yes?" Sheriff Linton said. He had a thin, alert face that was bisected by a full and well-kept black mustache. He was forty-five, perhaps, and affected an oversize ascot tie. He was as neat as new stovepipe and fully aware of it.

"Gentleman to see you, sir," the Negro boy told him.

"Send him in."

"There's a lady with him, sir. Out in the lobby."

Now Sheriff Ed Linton had learned the politician's first lesson: see everybody, listen to everybody and then use horse sense. He rose, excused himself and followed the boy out into the spacious red-carpeted lobby. It was more noisy out here, for mere glass windows could not shut out the brawling racket of the town's night life that flowed by on the streets outside.

The boy led him under the big crystal chandelier and across the lobby to a lounge in a corner and Sheriff Linton saw Ted Wallace and a rather beautiful girl rise to greet him. The disappointment over Ted Wallace, who was a relatively unimportant person in Pi-ute, was canceled out by the presence of the girl. Sheriff Linton put on his best smile, shook hands with Ted Wallace and then was introduced to Wallace's sister, Celia.

Erect, Ted Wallace was a carelessly dressed man in corduroy coat and levis. He was inches taller than his sister, and his hair was the same blond color. Only it was carelessly combed and wild, like the look on his long-jawed face. He might have been thirty, but the anger on his tanned face was the anger of a twelve-year-old.

"I've been trying to get you for two hours!" Ted Wallace said brusquely. "I want to report a robbery!"

Sheriff Linton nodded politely. "Take it to my chief deputy, Wallace. He's done some remarkable recovery of stolen articles."

"I'm not takin' this to any deputy," Ted Wallace said grimly. "I'm bringin' it to you, Linton. Layin' it on your lap. My sister was robbed of ten thousand dollars up in the pass last night. The stage was held up. I also know who did the job!"

The sheriff's eyes widened. "Too bad," he said, glancing at Celia. Her face was flushed with excitement as she watched Ted. "Now you say you know the robber?"

"Not the robber. The man who set him up to it." He paused. "It was Craig Armin who planned it and paid men to do it."

"Nonsense!" Sheriff Linton said immediately.

"That money," Ted went on implacably, "was for my freightin' business. It meant the difference between success and failure. I wrote to my sister for the money, and she answered, saying she was going to bring it out. She named the day and the amount."

"How do you suppose Armin knew that?" Sheriff Linton said, polite derision in his voice.

"I'm comin' to that. Those thug teamsters of his know every driver that carries mail into this town. My guess is that they bribed the mail drivers to open the sacks and run through the mail and read everything that was addressed to me. I know that"—Wallace's voice was really angry now— "because that letter from Sis had been opened. But when I got it it was too late to tell her to change her plans. She was robbed—and by Armin's men!"

"Prove it."

"Craig Armin's nephew, Cole Armin, was on the stage!"

"Proving exactly what?"

"That he was keeping an eye on her, pointing her out to the gunnies his uncle sent!"

"It's a neat theory," Linton admitted. "Proof's a different matter."

"Then get it!"

Linton smiled faintly. "Wallace, Craig Armin is a big name in this town. I can't accuse him of something like that without proof."

"Then get proof!" Wallace said curtly.

Linton inclined his head politely. "I'll try, I'll promise you that. It's only fair to state, however, that I don't believe he did it. Even if he did you couldn't get a jury to convict him. And chances are he'd turn around and sue you for false arrest and win his suit and ruin you." He shook his head. "Just between us, you'd better forget it. Don't ever fight a buzz saw."

"You mean you won't do anything about it?" Celia asked angrily.

Linton bowed. "On the contrary, I'll have my men work on it. I'm merely telling you what will happen. It's unfortunate, but it's so."

Ted Wallace glared at him, the anger of impotence in his face. Then he said quickly, "I'm not going to let you forget this, Linton. I'll be in your office three times a day. I'll turn this town upside down and shake it before I'll take that! Tell Craig Armin that! I'll get that money back if I have to blow up Monarch's safe!"

Linton bowed again. Ted Wallace took Celia by the arm and stalked out of the lobby. Behind them Sheriff Linton smiled crookedly, shrugged and reached in his pocket for a cigar on the way back to the bar. Such foolishness.

Out in the street, jammed in the river of humanity that flowed down the sidewalk, Ted Wallace strode protectingly beside his sister. He said suddenly, "I'll give him a week, and then I'll hold up the Monarch office and blow the safe!"

"Ted!" Celia cried. She looked up at him, and his face was grim. "They'd know!"

"Sure they'd know. Let 'em prove it though."

"But they could! Sheriff Linton was amused tonight. But if you hold up the Monarch he won't be amused any longer. He'd arrest you and the business would fall away and you'd lose everything you've done while you rotted in jail!"

"I will anyway."

"Oh, Ted. Isn't there any other way?"

"Not when you're fightin' pirates," Ted said gloomily.

They didn't talk after that. The office of the Western Freight Company—Ted Wallace's young and lusty freighting outfit—was on the main street, wedged between two stores. It was a narrow single room, originally built for an assay office. Behind it, wedged up tight against the back wall between it and the alley, was the wagon yard. It wasn't much, and when all the wagons were in—six in number—it was jammed. Across the alley in a fenced-in lot were the stables, the corral and the blacksmith shop. Above the office, in three small rooms, were Ted Wallace's quarters. To get to them it was necessary to walk down the alley and through the wagon yard and climb a shaky set of stairs.

It all looked mean and shoestring to Celia as she threaded her way through the high wagons in the yard, holding her skirts against her to keep the grease of the wheel hubs from smearing her. She knew it represented more money than was evident, but it was disheartening. Ted lived like an Indian, seldom slept, and then with one eye cocked to the safety of his wagons below his window. Given money, the money she had brought out with her, it might have been another story. But now it was hopeless. "Don't fight a buzz saw," Sheriff Linton had said. It was true, but she mustn't let Ted know. He must find that out for himself, find it out the hard way—by taking his licking. In the meantime she'd try and make these three inadequate rooms into a home of sorts for him.

When she mounted the stairs she found she was weary. Too much had happened, and it was all bewildering. Nothing counted here but violence and threats. Everything here was as harsh as the desert that started below the town and stretched out into a terrible fawn infinity.

She opened the door, her head hung with weariness and disappointment. Suddenly, a few steps into the room, a pair of boots came into her circle of vision. She started a little and looked up.

Cole Armin, still unshaven, with a livid bruise showing on his cheek beneath the beard stubble, was standing there with his hat in his hand.

"What are you——Ted, that's the man! Cole Armin!"

"I see him," Ted Wallace said softly. He shut the door behind him, and the three of them looked at each other. There was amusement in Cole Armin's face, but he said nothing.

Ted Wallace moved around the table in the middle of the room, pulling off his battered hat. "I'm goin' to have the pleasure of unscrewing the head of one of these Armins anyway," he said quietly.

Cole Armin smiled then. He made a gesture with his hat toward the table on which lay the canvas sack Craig Armin had given him. "Look that over before you swarm," he said mildly.

Celia went up to it, hefted it, caught the hint of what was in it and then swiftly untied the neck of the sack and dumped out its contents on the table.

She stared at it, motionless, and Ted Wallace came over slowly to gaze at it.

"The money," Celia whispered. "My money." She looked up at Cole Armin. "You—you're giving it back?"

Cole nodded. Celia stared at him and then at Ted, and then she ran around the table into Ted's arms. "Ted! Ted! It's our money! Don't you understand! Our money!" She shook him by the shoulders in her excitement and joy.

"I understand," Ted said slowly. He looked over her shoulder at Cole, his gaze puzzled and suspicious. "I understand that part of it. I still don't understand why you brought it back." There was the faintest suggestion of suspicion in his tone.

"I promised your sister I would," Cole said simply.

Celia turned to him then, her eyes still bright with excitement. "Did—did your uncle do it for you?"

Cole shook his head. He told them of his meeting with Juck and recognizing the anchor tattooed on his hand. He skipped any mention of the fight, merely saying that he used his recognition of Juck to blackmail the money out of his uncle.

When he was finished Celia said swiftly, "But you had a job! Will he give it to you now?"

"He couldn't give it to me. I wouldn't take it from a coyote like him," Cole said quietly.

"Tell us the rest of it," Ted Wallace said suddenly. "You've been in a fight."

"I had an argument with Juck."

Neither Ted nor his sister spoke, and Cole shifted his feet. "Well, I'll be goin'," he said.

"Wait a minute," Ted Wallace said. "You're through with that outfit of your uncle's then?"

Cole nodded.

Celia said, "What are you going to do?"

"Find a job."

Celia looked at Ted, and he looked at her. Something passed between them, something that didn't need speech to be understood. And then Ted Wallace smiled, and it was the first time Celia had seen him smile since she got here.

Ted said, "You aren't goin' to have to look very far for a job, Armin. How would you like to throw in with Western Freight?"

Celia was watching Cole, a deep pleasure in her green eyes. Cole's face was a study; surprise and bewilderment were there, and embarrassment too.

"You don't understand," Cole stammered. "This money ain't mine. It's yours. I just——"

"Returned it," Ted Wallace supplied. "You threw over a good job, rowed with your uncle, licked his plug-uglies and returned the money. That's enough for me. It'll save my life. I can get four more wagons now and more mules and teamsters and move into a new wagon yard and whip Craig Armin. I can use a man like you, and you can use a man like me. What about it? I mean it!"

Cole looked over at Celia and surprised an expression of eagerness on her face. She flushed a little and her glance dropped, but Cole knew she wanted him to say yes. But was it sensible? They were grateful to him now, this moment. Tomorrow they might regret their impulse. He didn't know anything about freighting. He was a cowman. He wasn't bringing anything—not even knowledge —to the business.

He said slowly to Ted, "But you don't know me, Wallace. And I reckon I don't savvy much about the business. I——"

"Forget it. I'll take a chance on the partnership if you will. What about it?"

Cole's unshaven face broke into a slow smile then, and his eyes were friendly. He liked Ted Wallace and Celia Wallace—and he needed a job. He was a stranger in a strange land, and these were his kind of people. He put out his hand and Ted took it warmly.

"Partners then?" Ted asked.

"I reckon we are," Cole said quietly. "If you want it that way."

There came a heavy knock on the door then, and Celia glanced at the money. Cole put his hand inside his coat and pulled out a gun and then looked over at Ted Wallace.

"Come in," Ted said.

The door opened, and a towering bulk of a man entered the room. It was Juck, hat in hand. His nose was swollen, his big mouth cut, and one eye was purple and closed. With the other he glanced at the three people there and his gaze settled on Cole.

"Friend Juck," Cole said dryly. "Come in and meet the girl you robbed."

Celia started in surprise and Juck came into the room, closing the door sheepishly after him. He was dusty and his shirt was stiff with dried blood, but there was no belligerence in his manner.

"I don't rightly know how to say this," he began, looking at Cole and then at Wallace. "I'm after a job, Wallace."

"Well, I'm damned!" Ted Wallace exploded. "You've got more gall than the mules you drive!"

"I know," Juck said. "Still, I'm a good teamster. I been fired from Monarch, kicked out. I—I can tell you, too, how I come to pull that robbery, if you'll let me talk."

"Let him talk, Ted," Celia said. "After all, he was nice to me— as nice as a stage robber can be, I suppose. He let me go into the bushes and take off my money belt when he found me after I'd run away."

"All right, talk!" Wallace said curtly. Cole just watched.

Juck shifted his feet. "Ain't much to say, I reckon. Armin told me if I'd do this holdup he'd give me Billings' job. Told me it was just a joke he was playin' on a woman friend of his. Said it didn't mean nothin' and that it was just for fun. When I told him I didn't like the idee he threatened to fire me. I got to figurin' if it was just for fun then there wasn't no sense in losin' my job over it. When I done it and give him the money he never fired that coyote Billings. He give me a bottle of whisky and told me to forget it." He glanced at Cole and fumbled with his hat. "I never knowed what it was all about until this here Texas man jumped me today. When I come to, Billings throwed me out in the street and kicked me."

Ted glanced over at Cole, and Cole knew that already, as his duty in a partnership less than ten minutes old, he was being con-

sulted and had to give his advice. He thought of something then
and said, "Juck, you've got to have work, haven't you?"

"I sure do. I can work," Juck said.

"There's another freightin' outfit in town, I heard Craig Armin
say. Name of Acme. Why don't you hit them for work?"

Juck fumbled with his hat some more. "I—well, I wanted to
work for Western."

"But why? If Miss Wallace wanted to she could get you tossed
into jail for months."

"I know that. Still—well, I just want to work for Western. Acme
is done for. They'll fold up. Western kin fight Monarch. Ted Wallace, well, he don't take it like Acme does. He fights. And I'm
honin' to get a crack at Monarch," Juck added grimly.

Cole looked over at Ted, and Juck, seeing that look, shook his
head. "Well, thanks for listenin' anyway. I don't s'pose I can do
nothin' if you want to arrest me."

"Wait a minute, Juck," Cole said. To Ted he said, "I think
you've got a good teamster if you can use him."

Ted nodded and said, "Juck, can you drive a ten-team hitch
down from the Glory Hole mine? Remember the road now before
you answer."

"I know the road. I'll do it in the dark. Better 'n that, I'll take a
ten-team hitch with an eighteen-ton load down from the China
Boy."

Ted Wallace laughed. "You're braggin', Juck."

"All right, call my bluff then to prove it. From the China Boy."

Ted looked over at Cole, who was grinning. Ted came around
the table and put out his hand. "Juck, you're hired. And you'll get
the toughest trick in Piute to drive, too, for that holdup."

"Suits me," Juck said. He grinned through swollen lips and
glanced over at Cole. "I know mules, mister. And them roads
don't come too tough for me. I'll be at work at six and you'll git
that ore hauled from me, never you worry."

He turned to the door and opened it. Going out, he paused and
looked back at Celia. "I'm right sorry about that rough handlin',
Miss Wallace. You want any mountains moved or mines dug or
armies licked you just call on me."

Celia laughed, and Cole knew then that she was not the kind of a
girl who could ever harbor vindictiveness. "All right, Juck. I'll
remember. Good night," Celia said.

Juck gone, Ted Wallace came over to the table and looked at the money. Then he glanced up at Cole and Celia, and his eyes were excited.

"Think of it," he said softly. "We can get contracts now that we couldn't get before, because we'll have the wagons. Cole, we're goin' to take the tough ones—the high mines like the Glory Hole and Swampscott—and the toughest of all, the China Boy. Armin won't touch 'em with a big wagon, and he doubles his rates when the going gets tough. We'll haul those mines with the big wagons and underbid him by a third. And when the rest of these mines hear about it they'll change outfits. Money is money, and they'll save it if they can."

"There'll be a fight," Cole said quietly. "I only met Craig Armin, but he hates like an Indian."

Ted Wallace's face sobered, and he nodded. "So do I." He looked at Cole and his gaze was level. "And so do you, partner, unless I'm blind."

Celia said matter-of-factly, "Then you two Indians put that money in the bag and sleep on it. I'm going to bed." She came up to Cole and put out her hand. "Thanks—for everything. If I'd known you better last night I would have known that your promise is really a promise and not talk."

Cole blushed and murmured something, and Celia turned to Ted. "You and Cole can sleep in the middle room on the cots. I'll sleep here on the couch. We can talk all this over in the morning."

Cole accepted the invitation, and Celia, the bag of money still in her hand, showed him into his and Ted's bedroom. It was a tiny affair partitioned off the corridor that connected the kitchen and the living room. She lighted the lamp and he saw two rough cots with clean blankets on them and a battered old dresser by the open window.

"And you can sleep on the money," Celia said, handing him the sack and smiling up at him. "You earned it."

He was just going to protest when there was a loud knock on the outside door and a voice shouted, "Open up!"

Celia stood motionless, staring at Cole. Cole was staring at her. They heard Ted unlock the door and the heavy scuffle of boots.

Then a voice said, "Put 'em up, Wallace! You're arrested! You'd better not make a move!"

And then, on the heel of that rough voice, came Sheriff Linton's silky drawl.

"You made a mistake, Wallace—a bad mistake. If you wanted to blow the Monarch's safe and steal ten thousand dollars you shouldn't have announced your plans to the sheriff. Where's the loot you got?"

4

For one brief instant Cole stood there, baffled. And then he was suddenly aware that he held ten thousand dollars in his hand—the ten thousand they would accuse Ted Wallace of stealing from the Monarch safe. He heard the swift tramp of feet coming toward them and Linton's voice saying, "Search the place!"

Cole moved then. He lunged for the window, swinging his leg over the sill. The noise he made was heard in the other room, for those feet began to run. "Be careful, Cole!" Celia cried.

In one desperate second Cole tried to remember what was below him, and he couldn't. He didn't know. He rammed the bag of money in his waistband, then swung outside, hanging from the sill. Then shoving himself away from the building with his foot, he dropped. It was only a six-foot drop to the sloping roof of the next building. He hit it, fell and started to roll down the roof to the passageway between the two buildings. He clawed wildly at the shake shingles and could not stop, and then he dropped off into space.

He hit the ground with a grunt and fell and rolled over on his back. A man's head appeared in the window above, and Cole lay motionless. The man put out a gun and shot, not down, but toward the rear of the passageway. Then he bawled, "He got away! Out the back stairs and you'll catch him!" And he poured three more shots toward the rear of the compound.

Cole came to his feet and ran for the street. He stepped out into the crowd that jammed the boardwalk and drifted with it for five minutes, until he was two blocks away. Whatever alarm they could raise now would take time. Besides, it would be like looking for a needle in a haystack. He was unknown here, save by a few people, and his description would be that of a tall man in a black suit who needed a shave.

He could fix that part of it up soon enough and give himself some time to think in the bargain. He drifted downstreet past the saloons where the barkers were standing, yelling in hoarse voices about the quality of the whisky and the girls inside, until he came to a barbershop. Spotting an empty chair, he went in, took it and asked the barber for a shave. The money bag against his belly was heavy, and it reminded him that he had to do something and do it fast. Once his face was lathered and the hot towel over it he knew he was as well hidden as if he were in the next state. And he considered.

This had all come so fast. In a few brief hours he had tossed one job overboard and won a partnership in Western Freight. He had learned that his uncle was crooked and bold as sin and that Celia Wallace and Ted Wallace were generous people. It embarrassed him and made him grateful at the same time. And before he had a chance to understand it all the law had broken into Ted's room to arrest him. Cole didn't understand much of it, only he was sure Ted Wallace hadn't blown the Monarch safe. And knowing Craig Armin the short time he had, he was willing to bet that Armin blew his own safe. Craig Armin wasn't wasting any time. He was going to ruin Western at the first chance, and this chance had come. Ted Wallace had unwisely made a brag and a protest to the sheriff, as Craig Armin knew he would. And now he would be jailed—the only man who could run Western Freight.

Cole's brain worked tirelessly while the barber shaved him. He wished savagely that he knew this town better, knew its people and its customs and the way it worked. Nothing he had learned in Texas applied to Piute. He couldn't break Ted out of jail, for that would outlaw them both and Western Freight would vanish. He knew one friendly man in this whole town—Juck. And he must work through him—and keep the money safe.

By the time the barber was finished Cole thought he had a plan. It was to match Craig Armin's gall with the same kind of coin.

"The saloons are doin' a right nice business tonight," he observed idly to the barber as he came out of the chair.

The barber, a mild little man with the face of a lugubrious undertaker, said, "They always do. Take all our money."

"Funny thing," Cole said, putting on his coat. "All these people —Mexicans and Irish and Germans—mixing together in one saloon. You'd think they'd fight all night."

"They don't mix," the barber said gloomily. "They each got their own favorite saloon."

"That a fact?" Cole said, looking in the mirror and putting on his hat. "I suppose they all like their own kind of people. Teamsters all hang out in one saloon, timbermen in another, hostlers in another, like that, eh?"

The barber nodded and said nothing. But Cole knew he was on the right track.

"What's the teamsters' bar, for instance?" he asked.

"The Desert Dust. Up a block and turn to your right." The barber made a face. "Phooey! It smells like they were servin' drinks in a stable. They're a tough lot too."

Cole smiled, waited until he was finished and then stepped out into the street. He let the crowd, which had thinned out somewhat on this edge of the business district, carry him along to the end of the block. Then he crossed the street, passed a second-rate saloon that was jammed to the doors and went up the side street. It was dark here, with a faint shaft of light up ahead.

When he reached that light he found that it was the Desert Dust. Its windows were dirty, and when he shouldered through the batwing doors into a bedlam of noise and smoke the stench of the stable hit him like a pillow. Squinting against the smoke, he walked down past the bar, crowded with rough and boisterous men in tattered clothes, and observed the drinkers. No luck. He passed on to the gambling tables in the rear then. And there, watching a faro game, was Juck, just as he had hoped he would be. He walked up to Juck and touched his arm. When Juck turned around he started with surprise at sight of Cole. Cole didn't say anything, only tilted his head toward the rear. Juck followed him out into the alley without a word.

Once outside and his eyes adjusted to the dark, Cole said, "Juck, I got ten thousand dollars in this bag. Can you hide it for me?"

"Sure," Juck said slowly, then added, "I don't get it, Armin. You mean you're trustin' me?"

"You're part of the company, Juck, and it's Western's money. You don't look like a man that'd steal."

"Give it here," Juck said roughly. "If I ain't got it when you want it I'll hang myself."

"That's only part of it. Now listen." He told Juck of the sheriff's visit, the arrest of Ted Wallace for blowing the Monarch's safe and his hunch that Craig Armin had blown his own safe to trap Ted Wallace with the money. Juck agreed that it was probable.

"All right, Juck. Now listen careful. I've thrown in with Ted Wallace. We're partners in Western. But I'm green in this town; I don't know anybody."

Juck nodded.

"I'm playin' a hunch now—shootin' in the dark. And you got to help me."

"What kin I do?"

"Before you promise to help me, Juck, there's something I want to tell you. You might go to jail for it."

"It's rough, hunh?" Juck asked.

"No. It's blackmail, Juck. Are you willin' to go to jail for that stage robbery of Celia Wallace?"

"Oh." Juck didn't say any more, and then Cole said quietly, "I don't think you'll have to, Juck. But you might. It's a risk."

"That's a long haul for robbin' a stage. You can't figure no other way?"

"No," Cole said. "There it is, Juck. If you don't want to take the chance say so."

Juck thought a moment and then said, "You take care of my family if I go?"

"I will," Cole said. "I'll promise it."

"Okay, then. Whut do I do?"

Cole smiled in the dark at this big man. He was simple and loyal, a good man.

Cole said, "Hide that money first. Then meet me at the Cosmopolitan House in fifteen minutes. That enough time?"

"Plenty," Juck said and vanished.

Fourteen minutes later Juck and Cole walked into the lobby of the Cosmopolitan House and inquired at the desk for Craig Armin's suite. It was 2-B on the second floor, and the clerk didn't think Mr. Armin wanted to be disturbed.

Cole ignored him and they went upstairs and found 2-B. They

were let into the foyer by a Chinese servant. Cole gave his name, knowing it would serve to draw Craig Armin from the party that was obviously going on in the rooms beyond. They were shown into a room off the foyer that was Craig Armin's elegantly paneled study.

They were scarcely seated in the rich deep chairs when Craig Armin came in. He was dressed in evening clothes, a wholly commanding man. He looked from Cole to Juck and back again and then said, "Well?" curtly, impatiently.

Cole came to his feet and said, "I'm plumb sorry about that robbery tonight, Craig, but I'm afraid you got the wrong man arrested."

Craig Armin shook his head. "The sheriff doesn't think so. Wallace made threats against me tonight, then robbed my safe."

"It's too bad," Cole sympathized. "Still, I think you better bail Wallace out."

"Bail Wallace out? Are you crazy?" Armin asked sharply.

Cole said obliquely, "Is Sheriff Linton in there?"

"Why—yes. He just got back from locking Wallace up." Armin smiled dryly. "And you want me to tell Linton to free him? You're a damned fool, my boy."

"Not free him," Cole said doggedly. "Just bail him out. Because if you don't bail him out Juck has a story to tell to the sheriff about a stage robbery."

Craig looked at Juck, understanding, and smiled faintly. "You like the idea of going to jail, Juck?"

"I'm all set for it." Juck grinned. "I'm gettin' paid to go. How about you? You all set for it?"

Craig's face changed slightly. "Nonsense! We both of us don't want to go."

"But Juck don't mind," Cole said softly. "He's willin'. All he's got to do is talk."

"I'll deny it!" Craig said sharply. "My word carries some weight."

"The only trouble with that is that you can't lie the numbers off bank notes," Cole lied calmly. "For instance, Miss Wallace had a one-hundred-dollar bank note, number A-177B34. Her bank wrote the number down back in Illinois. It is stolen from her by Juck, who admits it. It is returned to me by you. And she has it now. How did you get it unless Juck gave it to you?"

Craig Armin's face was tense. "That's bluff!"

"Not bluff," Cole said, "because your scheme didn't work, Craig. It would have worked if your pet sheriff had grabbed the money tonight and give it back to you. But he didn't. I've got the money and the bank notes." He turned toward the door and had his hand on the knob when he said, "I'll get the sheriff."

Craig Armin didn't move. He said, "Juck, I'll give you a thousand dollars to skip the country."

"To hell with you," Juck said promptly.

"Wait!" Armin said; then to Cole, "What's your price, Cole?"

"Bail Ted Wallace out."

"But, dammit, he's my competitor! How'll it look? He robbed my safe!"

"So he is. It's too bad." Cole smiled faintly at the rage and anger on Craig Armin's face. "You made one bad mistake, Craig. You figured Juck wouldn't want to go to jail and you were safe. I'll pay him to go to jail, just so he can drag you in too."

Craig Armin only glared at him.

"Understand," Cole said. "I'm not asking Linton to drop the charges. Linton wouldn't free him, because you played your hand too good. You couldn't make Linton free him without giving away your part in the robbery. But bail will get him out. Just put it on the line."

"You've got bail money!" Armin snapped. "Use it!"

"That money can't be spared, Craig. It's going for new wagons and mules so we can run you out of the country." He paused, grinning. "Well?"

Craig Armin's gaze sharpened. "We?" he echoed.

"I'm with Western—a partner," Cole said mildly.

Craig Armin's face settled into cold fury. He said slowly, "I'm willing to let bygones be bygones, Cole. Forget this nonsense, you and Juck, and come over to Monarch. We'll lick every freighting outfit in sight, and you'll have more money than you can spend."

Cole said, "I'll stay where I am, I reckon. I like the smell of my new partner considerable better than I do yours, Craig. And Juck likes his new boss better. We're goin' to have some fun, it looks like. We're goin' to see how far we can run you out of Piute." He grinned. "Now you aim to bail Wallace out?"

Without a word Craig Armin went to the door and Cole held it open for him. There was a look of savage hatred in Craig Armin's handsome face. He had been bested twice today by a cow hand from Texas, and he did not like it. But he was heading for Sheriff Linton right now and with bail money.

5

Cole did not enjoy his night's sleep in the hayloft of McFee's Livery Stable, but Juck didn't seem to mind. It had been necessary, however, because Cole was sure of one thing. Craig Armin, to wipe out the constant threat of having to answer for a stage robbery, would not rest until Juck—the man who could convict him—was dead. And Cole proposed to checkmate him as soon as possible.

Once the town was awake Cole left Juck in the loft, and without visiting the Wallaces he hunted up the most down-at-the-heels law office he could find. The firm of Chas. Beedle, Att'ny at Law, was located in a tent at the edge of town, one of a dozen such which housed the cheapest red-liquor joints in Piute.

Mr. Chas. Beedle had to be wakened from a drunken stupor. His office furniture consisted of a cot furnished with dirty blankets, a framed diploma, a stack of leather-covered law books and two jugs of his neighbor's best liquor. He was fat, unshaven and merry and didn't at all mind being wakened by Cole. Cole stated his business, and pen and paper were brought out. Cole dictated what he wanted drawn up into an affidavit. Leaving a blank space for the names, which Cole did not mention, the affidavit stated that Juck had robbed the stage at Craig Armin's request, had turned over the ten thousand dollars to Craig Armin and had been paid off with a bottle of whisky. Dates, times and such were as accurate as Cole could make them. He waited until Mr. Beedle, who showed no curiosity at all, had it copied out in the proper legal language and then waited some more for a duplicate. This was important. Afterward Cole paid him, bought him a drink at the neighboring tent saloon and went back for Juck.

Together they stepped into a hardware store next to the feed stable where there was a notary public. Both copies were filled in with the names and witnessed and notarized. Afterward Cole called for a sheet of paper and wrote a note. It was addressed to Craig Armin. It said:

> *In case you took a sudden dislike to Juck I am sending you this. It is a copy of the original affidavit, which is in the bank. As long as Juck stays healthy it will stay there. If anything happens to him I'll show it to the right people.*
>
> COLE ARMIN

He put the affidavit in an envelope and paid a boy a dollar to deliver it to Craig Armin's suite. After that, breathing easier, he sent Juck off to get the cached money and headed upstreet for the Western Freight Company offices—his office, he suddenly realized.

It was a bright day, and yesterday's heat seemed still to cling to the dust of the busy street. For the first time since he had arrived he took a close look at the town. From now on this was his town, and it would make him or break him. In a month men would be nodding to him with a respect shown an equal or else laughing at him. He liked the idea somehow. It appealed to the stubborn streak in him, and when he turned into the compound of Western Freight he was smiling.

The compound was deserted of all wagons except one. Cole climbed the steps and knocked on the door of the Wallaces' living quarters, and Celia opened the door.

An involuntary cry of delight and relief escaped her, and then she smiled and he went in. Ted Wallace, stripped to the waist, was shaving, the small mirror propped up in the window. He said, grinning, "Hi, boy," and looked at Celia. "Satisfied?" he asked.

"Of course," Celia said. Color crept into her face, and she looked prettier than ever.

Cole wore a look of puzzlement, and Ted explained: "Sis has been in a stew half the night and all morning. About you, Cole. She was afraid something had happened to you."

"Well, he didn't come back here," Celia protested. She was still blushing and Ted grinned at her, then said to Cole, "I told her any man who could jump out a window with ten thousand dollars, dodge the sheriff and talk Craig Armin into goin' my bail—well, nothin' could happen to him."

"He bailed you out then?" Cole asked.

Ted nodded and his smile faded a little. "Bailed out, for five thousand. My trial's next month. In that time," he said slowly, "I've got to find proof that I didn't blow his safe. There's one way to do that. Just run him out of the country. And now," he asked finally, "how did you swing it?"

Cole sat down and told them what argument he had used to persuade Craig Armin to go Ted's bail and what he had done that morning to keep Juck alive. By the time he was finished Juck came in with the money, and then Celia called breakfast for them.

Ted put on a black suit and came out just as they were finishing. "Juck," he said, "you know a good ore wagon when you see one. And, Cole, you know good mules. This morning you and Juck buy four big wagons, tandem, and eighty mules. The Acme Freight outfit will be glad to get rid of 'em. Me, I'm goin' over to the Cosmopolitan House to see Huggins." To Cole he explained: "He's manager of the Glory Hole mine. He can't get enough ore out because the mine is too high for the big wagons. Monarch won't use them on that road. They're scared. This afternoon, Juck, you're goin' to haul eighteen tons of ore in one load down from the Glory Hole to Union Milling. If you get down without a broken neck, smashed wagons and twenty dead mules we've got the contract."

"I'll do it," Juck said and grinned through his thick lips. "When I git down with that I'll take the same hitch down from the China Boy."

"What is this China Boy?" Cole asked.

Ted shook his head and laughed ruefully. "It's a mine the end of the world, higher than the sky, and the birds are scared to perch on the road to it. If we get the Glory Hole contract we're goin' after that."

"One thing at a time," Juck said, and Ted laughed then.

Ted turned to Celia. "Sis, I've even got a job for you. Go over to Simmons and buy out his lumberyard and his ground this mornin'. Western's gettin' a new wagon yard too. I'll be ready to sign the papers this noon." He looked at Cole. "That all right with you, partner? Here goes our ten thousand."

Cole grinned. "It's all right with me," he agreed. "I don't savvy it much, but I'm for it." As a partner in a freighting business Cole found he had a lot to learn about it.

There were several roads out of Piute—rough, sandy and rocky

—but only one of them went very far. That led over the Sierras and into California, while the rest led to the mines high up on the shoulders of the Sierra Negras. Most of the mines in the Piute field had been forced by the location of the gold-and silver-bearing ore strata to pitch on the craggy heights a thousand feet above the flats.

Cole and Ted, riding in front of the high-sided ore wagons in tandem that Juck was driving, looked at them now. To their left were the mountains, scarcely timbered on this eastern slope, sharp and black and frowning. They rose in almost sheer, dipping, tilting, rearing ramparts beyond the town, challenging the ingenuity of the mine founders in getting their mine buildings to even stay put on the steep slope. Cole pointed them out, one by one, tiny clusters of corrugated-roofed buildings with a long heap of tailings smeared below them.

To Cole's right, out on the flats, were the reduction mills. In the still, hot desert out here the boom of their stamps kept the air pulsing. Seven of them lay sprawled in huge red buildings across the face of the rolling rocky waste below the town. Here was the problem laid out for any man to see. It was to get the most ore in the least number of trips for the least amount of money down that two-thousand-foot drop to the reduction mills. A railroad, still new to the West in this year, 1873, could not do it, so mules had to. And the man who had the wagons and the courage to keep that ore moving had his hand on the throat of the Piute field.

When the road turned toward the mountains Juck shaded his eyes and peered up. The narrow road, crawling in switch-backs up the face of the slope, was shared by three mines, the Elfin, the Swampscott Girl and the Glory Hole, one above the other, the Glory Hole highest of all. Since the road was a one-way affair a system of signals had been devised. When a loaded wagon pulled into the narrow opening beside the Elfin building a huge red flag, visible to the freighters on the flats, was hung out. It meant that a wagon was on its way down, and until it was on the flats no up traffic was allowed. When Juck looked there was no red flag.

At the foot of the lifting road Ted said to Cole, "You go on up with Juck. I'm headin' over for the Union Milling to see about some more mules. I'll catch up with you before you get to the Glory Hole." He pulled his horse aside and then added, "Go ahead of Juck, and you'll be out of the dust."

Cole waved and rode on. He spurred his horse, pulled past Juck who was cursing out his half-broken mules for the long haul, and then he was on the road. It lifted in a sharp grade, clinging to the face of the black rock. Soon it made a switchback, and to Cole's inexperienced eye it seemed an impossible space for two big wagons in tandem to negotiate. The road lifted steadily, making countless switchbacks. And now it was high, with the sheer drop to the canyon below an ever-present threat. The road had been blasted out of living rock at an enormous cost of time and powder, but when Cole came to one switchback he reflected that both more time and more powder should have been expended on it. It was narrow and sudden, and one slip would send a team hurtling down six hundred feet to annihilation on the rocks below. He rode past it and then turned in his saddle to see how Juck would negotiate it.

Juck's lead team swung wide, almost to the cliff's edge, and then the others came on, nimbly skipping the taut chain as it crowded into the wall. And then the swing team came in sight, pulling straight for the edge, and finally the wheel team, with Juck mounted on the off mule. He held his mule close to the edge, watching the stub of the tongue, and then suddenly the wagon came in sight. Its hub missed the rocks by two feet, and Cole grinned at his own concern. Juck had done it without a pause.

Cole swiveled his head back to look up the trail, and there, forty feet ahead of him, halted on the trail, was a new buckboard pulled by a team of horses.

Cole reined up, the rumble of the empty wagons swelling behind him, and he saw who was in the buckboard. It was Keen Billings and another man.

Keen Billings had his gun drawn and pointed at Cole.

The rumble of the ore wagons stopped and Cole could hear the heavy breathing of the lead mules behind him, and then Juck clamped the brakes on. Keen Billings was grinning, his big muscular jowls knotted in a smile.

"Hullo, Nephew," Keen drawled. "Funny place to meet, ain't it?"

Juck's voice lifted in the following silence. "Keen, back that damn team up and clear out of here! Where was your flag?"

Keen handed his gun to the other man and dismounted on the wall side of the road; the space between the buckboard and the drop side of the road was too narrow for comfort. He walked past his team and stopped in front of Cole.

"So you're the hard-case freighters who aim to freight the Glory Hole stuff with a ten-team hitch, eh?"

Cole folded his arms and leaned on the saddle horn. "That's right."

"You need practice, maybe," Keen said, laughter in his eyes.

"That's why we're here."

"All right. Practice backin' that hitch down to the flats. You listenin', Juck?"

Juck was. He yelled, "Damn you, Keen, you can't do that! There's a clause in every contract Craig Armin has got that says if he don't obey flag signals the contract is void!"

"That's right," Keen said smoothly, "Only read it again. It don't mention any buckboards, does it? Maybe you didn't notice. I'm drivin' a buckboard, not an ore wagon."

"We got right of way over that!"

"Take it if you can," Billings retorted. He laughed deep in his throat. "This ought to be good. Go on back to the flats, Juck. I'd like to see it done."

The situation was clear enough to Cole. Juck couldn't come up to back any play Cole might make. If Juck dismounted and tried to walk on the off side of his spans one shot from the gunnie in the buckboard would frighten the mules and Juck would go over. If he tried to walk between them or on the cliff side that same shot would get him kicked to death by the mules. Keen Billings knew it, too, and he was enjoying it. Juck was helpless back there, cursing in his impotence. Cole had to do something and do it quickly, and he could think of nothing except stalling.

"Look, Billings," Cole said swiftly. "A couple of hundred dollars ought to make you change your mind."

"A thousand wouldn't," Keen Billings said, laughing. "Go ahead and sweat blood for a while. I'd like to see it."

Cole drew out a sack of tobacco from his shirt pocket and rolled a smoke, watching Keen. He cursed himself for having come along without a gun. And he wondered what would happen if he would sink spurs in his horse. Nothing, probably, except the horse would rear up and Keen would back off. But what if there were some way to get the horse to lunge into Keen, surprising him?

He lighted and took a deep drag from his cigarette, and he thought he had it.

Keen was grinning at him, and Juck was silent, too concerned to curse.

"I might raise the ante above a thousand," Cole drawled. He extended his sack of tobacco lazily. "Smoke? It's a peace-pipe smoke, Billings."

"Not from you it ain't," Billings said curtly. "No, thanks."

Cole still held the sack of tobacco out and said, smiling a little, "The Indians scalp a man for turnin' down the peace pipe. Don't go against your luck."

Gently he pulled his horse around so it was quartering to Billings.

Billings was laughing. "I ain't an Indian, Nephew. I don't smoke with you not ever."

"Okay," Cole said and started to pocket his tobacco. At the same time, fighting the distaste for the job, he crushed his burning cigarette into the shoulder of his horse. The horse's instinctive reaction, as he guessed it would be, was to shy away from the pain. And that meant that he lunged forward and sideways, into Keen Billings.

Three things happened then. Cole rolled out of his saddle toward Billings; Billings yelled and lunged back, and the gunnie on the buckboard let go with a shot.

The slug missed Cole and hit his horse squarely in the head. Cole, his lunge falling short, knew he would miss Billings, but the pitch of the falling horse added to his momentum as he rocketed out of the saddle; his shoulders slammed into Billings' knees. Billings went over backward, kicking. Over the racket Cole could hear Juck cursing the frightened mules.

And then both he and Billings were down, almost under the feet of the buckboard's team. Cole knew that he was screened from the man with the gun for several seconds, and he ducked his head against the awkward drubbing Billings was giving him from flat on his back.

Savagely then Cole pulled himself toward Billings' head and brought his elbow crushingly into Billings' face. Billings grunted and put his hands up to his bleeding mouth. Raising his fist like a hammer, Cole pounded it down on Billings' thick nose. For seconds then the fight was gone out of him. Cole rolled to his knees, yanked Billings up by the slack of his shirt to his knees, bending his arm around behind him, and then hauled him to his feet, facing the gunnie. Cole was behind Billings, shielded by him.

"Go ahead and shoot!" Cole taunted the gunnie.

The man was standing on the bed of the buckboard, reins of the skittish horses in one hand, the gun in the other. And he couldn't shoot.

Cole said swiftly, "Throw that gun away!"

"Damned if I will!" the man yelled. "Let him go!"

Cole shoved Billings straight at the head of the nearest horse. The smell of blood, the cursing and the violence frightened the horse. He reared back, and the buckboard slewed around, its hind wheel on the edge of the drop.

"Throw that gun behind me!" Cole yelled.

The gunnie took one terrified look at the rear wheel of the buckboard and yelled: "Quit it! I'm goin' over!" In his fright he had forgotten the gun.

"Throw it over here or I'll shove you off!" Cole yelled.

The gunnie was licked. He tossed the gun over the horses, and Cole shoved Billings to his knees and lunged for it. He came up with it in his palm. The gunnie had driven the horses up out of danger. And Billings, his nose streaming blood and his eyes watering, came sullenly to his feet, facing Cole. Juck let out a whoop of joy. He was halfway down the chain; all thought of the danger of being kicked vanished at the sight of Cole's predicament. Now he vaulted to the back of the closest mule and yelled: "Steady, Cole. I'm comin'."

Cole drawled to Billings, "Want to see how a worm turns, Billings?"

He looked up just in time to see the gunnie vanish over the tail gate of the buckboard and run up the road.

Juck pounded up behind Cole. "Unhitch that team, Juck," Cole said.

Juck made a fast job of it. Cole said then, "Billings, give him a hand. Take that front wheel. When I count three you heave."

Juck chuckled, sensing what was going to happen. He took the rear wheel, Billings the front. At the count of three they heaved, and the buckboard made a slow turn on its off wheels, hung there a second on its side, then toppled over the cliff. None of them spoke, waiting the seconds until they heard the crash of the buckboard hundreds of feet below on the rocks.

Cole said, "Now, Juck, we'll get my dead horse off the same way."

Billings and Juck rolled Cole's dead horse off the edge, first taking off the saddle and bridle.

"And now, you loudmouthed joker," Cole said slowly to Billings, "You're goin' to see something. Saddle one of those horses for me. Drive the other up the road ahead of you. You're goin' to walk. You're goin' to walk clear up to the Glory Hole. We'll load this wagon and you're goin' to ride on top of the load down this road. There's a chance Juck can't make it and he'll lose the load. And if he does you'll make almost as big a splash as the mules. Now git, mister!"

Keen Billings presented himself at suite 2-B of the Cosmopolitan House at nine o'clock that night weary to exhaustion, his feet blistered, his clothes covered with dust and still not wholly over his fright. He stumbled into Craig Armin's office, and when Armin came in Billings was sitting in a chair, boots off his bleeding feet, his head hung.

Armin closed the door behind him and surveyed Billings with distaste. "Now what?"

Billings told him what had happened. Cole Armin, Juck and Ted Wallace, not content with beating him up and destroying the buckboard, had walked him to the Glory Hole, then made him ride down atop eighteen tons of ore to the Union Milling, from which place they had made him walk back to town.

"And what do you want of me?" Craig Armin asked dryly when Billings was finished.

Billings' mouth gaped. He was confounded for the moment. "Why—I thought you'd want to know."

"What a fool I've got for a super!" Armin said scathingly. He walked over to his desk and handed Billings the Piute *Enterprise*. "Read that!" he said savagely. "And when you're done with that read this!" He took another paper from his desk top and slapped it on the newspaper that Billings had taken.

Billings first read the newspaper story. It asked, with a successful attempt at sly humor, why Craig Armin had bailed out his competitor from jail after said competitor had robbed his safe. The other paper was Cole's affidavit, along with the note.

Billings looked up, not knowing what to say.

"And you expect me to cry over your little prank kicking back?" Craig Armin asked in a cold fury. "Why, damn you, Billings, I had this business built up to where I didn't have to worry! I could forget it! But now you botched up the whole thing. Why did Juck ever leave that yard alive? Why didn't you get him before he could get to Wallace? Why did you ever fire him in the first place? And why didn't you tell me all this? What in the name of hell do you think I pay you for?"

"I—I couldn't see how it'd turn out," Billings stammered.

"Maybe this will help you see!" Armin raged. "I'm not firing you, Keen. I'm cuttin' your wages in half! Furthermore, I'm going to sign a contract with the China Boy for a price that Western can't match! And you—you've got to come through with teamsters and guts enough to get that ore down in big wagons!" His face was livid with rage. "I want this Western run out of Piute! We'll beat their prices if we have to lose money on it! And it's up to you to get out the stuff! You hear? It's up to you! *You!* No more choosing and picking the low mines! We're goin' up for ore from the high mines! If I don't get that China Boy contract—if you can't swing it—then we'll wreck Western! I don't know how, but we'll do it! *You'll* do it, you hear? *You!*"

He ceased talking, breathing heavily. Then he said in a calm voice, "Get out! You stink!" He walked out of the room, closing the door carefully behind him.

6

Back in his room at one of the more modest of Piute's hotels, Keen Billings threw himself on his bed. He had a bottle of whisky and a water tumbler in his hands, and he shakily poured himself a half tumbler of liquor and drank it down. He sat there, waiting for the glow to start in his belly, listening to the night sounds of the town outside his window. A cold fury seemed to have frozen his brain. All he could think of at present were Craig Armin's last words: "Get out. You stink."

Presently he rose, stripped his shirt off and poured out a basin of water, first taking another drink. He washed, the whole scene in Armin's suite simmering in his mind. So he was a dog, was he? He'd been running Craig Armin's dirty errands for three years now, fronting for his shady work, bluffing deputies, buying off the law, using his bully boys and blackmailing when they wouldn't work. And for all this he was getting his pay cut in half and being driven to suicidal work. For he knew, well as he knew his name, that not a teamster in Monarch's pay would take a ten-team hitch down from the China Boy unless he did it first. And he couldn't do it. He couldn't take that hitch down from the Glory Hole like Juck had done today, much less from the China Boy. The thought of it put goose-pimples on the skin of rope-muscled shoulders. He was through at the Monarch when he refused that job. And he would refuse. He had to.

He sat down on the bed again, feeling physically better. But anger was having its way with him. He hated that Western crew, every man jack of them, but it was a professional hatred. His hatred for Craig Armin was hot and wicked and overpowering. If he had the nerve he would like to kill him. But he didn't. Still it was either kill him or get killed himself. Keen Billings cursed with the passion of a maniac, and when he got that out of his system he started to think.

Presently he got up and put on a clean shirt and combed his short black hair. His eyes, when he looked at them in the mirror, were crafty, and he smiled at that. Damned right they were crafty. He had an idea.

He put on a coat, took a last drink, which brought the bottle to a third full, then put the bottle under his pillow. Because he was going where he was he got out his best Stetson.

At the bar of the Cosmopolitan House he took his drink over to an empty table and sat down. His nose felt as big as an apple where Cole Armin had smashed it, but it couldn't be helped. He kept his eyes on the door, watching the movement of the customers. Presently, as he had hoped, Sheriff Ed Linton walked into the room, looking around him for company. He saw Keen, nodded and pretended to ignore Keen's beckoning finger.

Keen had to go to the bar and say, "Bring your drink over, Ed. You and me have got medicine to make."

Cornered thus, Sheriff Linton couldn't demur, although Keen Billings was not a good man to be seen with. Too rough.

Seated at the corner table, Keen leaned back. "I think you and me ought to pool a little information, Ed."

"I doubt it," Sheriff Linton said coldly. He didn't want to be too familiar with this Billings, and his eyes said so if his words didn't.

Billings understood him, but he was not one to be snubbed. "You know, I can remember when you were an out-at-the-pants shyster over in Marysville," Billings drawled. "The boys used to throw you out of the saloon just for fun."

"Is that what you called me over for?" Sheriff Linton said coldly.

"Hunh-unh. I called you over to talk about money. Big money."

"How much?" Sheriff Linton asked idly.

"Say a couple hundred thousand."

Sheriff Linton's eyes lighted with interest, but it was cautious interest.

"You never saw that much," he sneered.

"How would you like the Monarch Freighting Company and all of its contracts?" Billings said bluntly.

Linton stared at him for a long moment, many things streaking through his mind. He said only, "Big talk."

"Okay," Billings said indifferently. "Go 'way."

Linton didn't stir, only looked at Billings. "Go on. I'm listening."

"So you can tell Craig Armin maybe?"

"I know when to keep my mouth shut. I said go ahead."

"Armin ain't so tough," Billings said quietly. "He can be cracked wide open. He *is* goin' to be cracked wide open," he corrected. "Question is, after he's cracked who's going to take his place?"

"The Western?"

Keen Billings said softly, "If we don't."

Linton looked around him and hitched his chair closer. "You interest me. Go ahead."

Billings said, "You want it with the bark on or off?"

"Get to it, man!" Linton said impatiently.

Billings hunched over the table and began to talk in a low voice.

"Craig Armin has got his fight up, Ed. He's out to lick Western any way he can. Tonight he told me he's goin' to make another try for that China Boy contract. That shows how much he means business."

"Can you swing it?"

Billings grinned. "Don't get ahead of me. I say Craig Armin aims to fight. If he can't beat Western aboveboard he'll wreck 'em. That give you any ideas?"

"Not many."

"It does me. What if I lose this China Boy contract for him? What if we can't swing it? What if I lose other contracts for him? Can't get the ore out, and he has to forfeit. What if I lose mules for him—and wagons and men—so that these mines won't give Monarch any business? And all the time it will look like an accident, like Western was gettin' rough. What will he do?"

"What will he?"

"I tell you, he'll fight Western! And when he's crowded far enough he'll give me orders to wipe out Wallace and Armin. That's the way he plays, Ed—beat 'em or kill 'em."

"I see," Linton said slowly. "Then what?"

"When Wallace and Armin are dead," Billings said slowly, "we make him our proposition. He hired Wallace and Cole Armin killed. I've got the proof, because my men and me will do it. He robbed Celia Wallace of ten thousand. I've got the proof. He blew his own safe to land Ted Wallace in jail. I've got the proof, because I blew the safe."

Linton's eyes widened, but he said nothing.

"We—you and me—put that up to him," Billings said grimly, "and then give him his choice. He signs Monarch over to us and clears out of Piute, or we arrest him, jail him and hang him." Billings leaned back and spread his hands. "What's simpler? I got the evidence; you got the authority. I tell you, Monarch is ours for the takin'—yours and mine!"

Sheriff Ed Linton's face was a strange thing to see then. As a politician he had learned to school his emotions, but now naked greed mounted in his eyes. There was first caution, then interest, then dismay, then calculation, then approval, tinged with doubt.

He said slowly, "All right as far as it goes, Keen. But if you pull down Monarch until Craig'll fight you'll build up Western at the

same time. And when we get Monarch—if I go in with you, I mean
—we'll have a dead horse—not worth a damn."

"Wrong!" Billings said flatly. "Didn't I say Craig would tell me
to get rough with Western? Don't worry. I'll wreck 'em. I'll whittle
'em down to our size before Craig is crowded into makin' his play.
And then, without Cole Armin or Ted Wallace to run it, we can
buy 'em out for drink money."

"It's nice if you can do it," Linton conceded slowly. "But those
two are tough hombres."

"I'll have someone in their office," Billings said quickly. "They
can't make a move but what we know it."

"That," Linton said dryly, shaking his head, "is the first nonsense you've talked, Keen."

Billings leaned forward eagerly. "Some time ago Monarch had a
teamster, name of Pete Burns. Young fella, proud, educated, and
he was savin' money to go to medical school back East. The boys
had a grudge agin' his uppity ways, so they loosened a kingbolt on
his wagon. He come down from the Lord Peter with a load and the
wagon broke loose. He broke both legs and got gangrene and died.
To cover it up I told his sister it was some of Ted Wallace's work.
She hates Wallace more than anything in this world." He tapped
his finger on the table for emphasis. "That gal is beautiful. She's
smart. She also knows how to keep books."

"I don't follow you," Linton said slowly.

"Haven't you heard that Ted Wallace bought out old Simmons'
lumberyard next to his corral behind the Western office this morning?"

"No. Besides, what's that got to do with it?"

Billings laughed shortly. "He'll need a bookkeeper. Letty Burns
will be that bookkeeper. And best of all, Craig Armin will pay her
to spy for us, because he figures it will help him."

"A woman?"

"You haven't seen her or heard her talk. She'll get the job." He
leaned back in his seat now, surveying the sheriff. "There's the
proposition, Ed—colder than turkey. Between us we can take care
of Craig Armin. Our only worry is that Western will have all the
contracts when we get Monarch. I say they won't. I say, with this
gal to tip us off to their moves, we can keep them broker than
Monarch." He smiled slowly. "Find a hole in that if you can." He
added quietly, "You can't. Monarch is ours for the takin'."

Sheriff Linton built a steeple with his fingers and stared at it in heavy concentration. Billings watched his face and saw the greed mount up in his eyes. He had chosen his man with care, for Ed Linton was hungry for money—as hungry as Keen was for revenge. A half-smile played on Sheriff Linton's face for a long minute, and then his eyes grew skeptical.

"It's a nice scheme, Keen—but for one thing."

"What's wrong with it?"

"You say Craig Armin, before he will take a licking, will kill Cole Armin and Ted Wallace."

"He will."

"How do you know he will? There's a lot of difference between fighting and killing, Keen—a lot of difference. Armin doesn't strike me as a man who'll order murder."

Keen Billings' smile was slow, wicked. "Ed, just how do you think old man Joyce—the fellow who owned Acme freight—died?"

"Why, his horses spooked on a high mountain road and he fell off the cliff."

Billings shook his head. "I shot him," he said simply. "Armin paid me to."

Linton's eyes glinted, and he leaned back slowly in his chair. He sized up Keen Billings a long moment, weighing the man, and then he snapped his fingers. "Boy!" he called.

When the bar boy came over Linton said, "I want a look at your wine list." As the boy went to get it Linton said to Billings, "That's all I wanted to know, Keen. It's a deal. And we'll drink to success in champagne. Because I think we've got something here."

They shook hands, firmly and hard.

7

At the end of his first day's work behind a ten-span hitch Cole had a deep respect for Juck's ability. He swung his team up toward the hoppers of the Union Milling and found two wagons ahead of him.

Pulling up his teams in the dusk, he turned and waved Ted Wallace, who was behind him, to a halt, then dismounted stiffly. He was tired, his nerves edgy, for he was not used to this work. He had been freighting from the Lord Peter all day, but even its wide road and its gentle grade had been hard enough for him. He had a lot to learn, he thought humbly, before those tons of ore behind him ceased to be a constant threat.

He was slapping the dust from his Stetson when Ted Wallace walked up.

"Aren't those Monarch wagons at the hoppers?" Ted asked.

Cole glanced over in the dusk, saying he didn't know.

"Since when did they start freightin' in spring wagons?" Ted asked contemptuously and then added, "Let's have a look."

The small wagons were half empty now. Their ore was being shoveled into the big hoppers which were located on the highest point of the slope above the descending buildings of Union Milling. Fed down by gravity, it would soon be in the mill's stamps, which were making the evening dusk throb even now.

The tally man from the mill and some idle shovel men stood around the wagons, grinning. The Monarch teamster was standing by the front wheel of his wagon, scuffing the dust with his feet.

As Cole and Ted approached Cole saw his relief man, Bill Gurney, squatting on the road to the side of the teamster. Bill was talking, and Cole put a hand on Ted's arm as they mingled with the shovel men and paused to listen.

Bill Gurney was a sour little monkey, rough-tongued and hard-bitten and scrappy. He was saying to the teamster, "Tell me again, Loosh. It give me an earache the first time."

The Monarch teamster looked over at him and said, "Go easy, rooster. You're liable to loose some teeth."

"You won't loosen 'em," Gurney said promptly. "You ain't got a man in your outfit that could hit the ground with his hat. Not after today you ain't. You're dead, the hull damn lot of you."

The Monarch teamster flared up. "Okay, runt. You'll have a crack at it pretty soon, I reckon. See if you can do better."

"We'll do better," Gurney said. "We just got the nerve. We're gettin' paid wages. We ain't bein' drove. We're gettin' a bonus. We got good mules and harness. We'll do it."

"Maybe," the tally man from the mill said.

The Monarch teamster looked over at him and nodded agreement. "Maybe is the word. Me, I don't think it can be done."

Gurney said dryly, "Not by them Monarch women it can't. You're damn right."

Loosh lunged for him then. Bill stepped back, came to his feet, and he held a heavy wagon spoke in his hand. Loosh stopped at sight of it. "See that," Gurney said, waving the spoke. "I can wrap that around your skull, Loosh, if I wanted to. Now look." He threw the wagon spoke away, and when he spoke his voice was sharp with scorn. "I don't need nothin' to whup you, Loosh. You and your hull damn lot. Come on."

Cole said quietly, "Easy, Bill. What's the ruckus?" and stepped into the circle of men. The shovel men in the wagon had ceased work now and were watching.

Bill swiveled his head, saw Cole and grinned. "Howdy, Cole." He nodded his head toward the enraged teamster. "Ain't you heard?"

"What?"

"Monarch got a wagon hung up on the China Boy road this mornin'. Not a man in the lot of 'em, includin' Keen Billings, had the guts to drive her down. So they unhitched and shifted the load to these damn buggies, and it's took 'em seven hours to get the load down." He looked over at Loosh and grinned. "That's right, ain't it, Loosh?"

"You'll get a crack at it!" Loosh snarled. "Let's see how you do it!" He turned and walked away. Bill laughed and went over to Cole's wagon, and Cole walked over to Ted.

"You heard him?"

"Sure," Ted said slowly.

"You thinkin' the same thing I am?"

Ted nodded. They were both thinking, not of the Monarch's failure, but of their chances. Ever since the Piute field was established the China Boy, a fairly rich mine, had been forced to shut down time and again because its ore could not be moved fast enough to keep men in work. Its isolation, its height, the treacherous shale that the road to it passed through had all combined to scare out the freighters. Small wagons could move it, but it took too many wagons, horses and men, and the cost of them made the freighting prohibitive. There was a standing offer by the super of the China Boy that any outfit who could move four hundred tons of ore in a day would get a contract that was better than any offered in the Piute field. And the only way to move those four hundred tons of ore was in big wagons, tandem.

Ted Wallace, like Cole, was mentally calculating their chances. With their four new wagons they had ten now, all told. By working from dawn to dusk, pulling all wagons off the other jobs, including the new Glory Hole job they'd just landed, they could, by making two trips with twenty tons to a wagon, deliver the four hundred tons. The Monarch had tried and failed. Up till now Ted Wallace had never had the wagons. He had them now, and this was the time to make his bid. Craig Armin, thinking to cut him out by getting the contract first, had failed to move the required ore.

Ted said finally, "I think we've got a little business to talk over with the China Boy super tonight, Cole. Let's ride."

It had been a punishing day, for they were crowding their luck. Riding back in the dusk, Cole could see the lights of Piute winking ahead of him. The setting sun, long since screened out by the hulking mass of the Sierra Negras, put the town in darkness early. Piute lay there under the shoulder of the mountain, challenging them to lick it.

Already, Cole reflected, the money Celia had brought was spent. It had been poured into wagons, into more and better mules, into harness and into a new wagon yard, which was started that morning. They were taking chances, he and his new partner. They were betting on doing a hard job better than Craig Armin and trusting to luck and skill to pull them through to their reward.

Ted looked over at Cole, who was silently contemplating the town. "You feel a little funny in the stomach?" Ted said.

Cole looked at him and shook his head slowly. "I don't reckon, why?"

"That China Boy business," Ted said wryly. "A man's a fool to try it. But if we swing it we'll have a contract that will let us buy ten more wagons and two hundred more mules. And with that, Cole, we're on top. We'll have this field tied up." He shook his head and murmured, "But what a hell of a chance!"

"You've got the drivers, ain't you?" Cole asked.

"Countin' myself, yes."

"Then we'll swing it," Cole answered. "The only thing I don't like is that you're takin' the chances, Ted. I'm not. I didn't put up any money. And I can't drive a wagon good enough to help out."

Ted laughed then, his uncertainty gone. "Did you ever stop to think, partner, that if you hadn't been thinkin' a little faster than Keen Billings yesterday we'd only have nine wagons today? And with nine wagons we couldn't even try for the China Boy contract."

It was slight compensation to Cole, however. Yesterday he had been lucky. Maybe he wouldn't be again. And all the time there was that thought in the back of his mind that it was Celia Wallace's gratitude and Ted Wallace's generosity that were responsible for his being in Western Freight. He wasn't pulling his share of the load, it seemed to him. And his willingness to learn the business and share the work was, in the end, not much more than just willingness. Any six-dollar-a-day teamster could do his work and do it better than he could.

It was dark when they rode into Piute. They avoided the main street, clinging to the off streets where mean little shacks housed the shifting population.

They turned into the alley that ran between the corral and office, and Cole found himself eager to see how the day's work on the new yard had progressed. There was a lantern in the old corral and wagon yard when they rode in. Along one side of it, rank on rank, mules were chewing contentedly at their feed. The board fence on the other side of the lot adjoining the lumberyard had been torn away, and a long stretch of new board fence loomed up in the dark.

They unsaddled, turned their horses to water in the pole corral at the rear of the yard by the stables.

Together, then, they walked over into the new wagon yard, pausing by the edge of the stables to look into it. There wasn't much to see in the darkness. The lumber sheds had been torn down, and the boards were piled over the lot. The new board fence had been hastily thrown up around both old and new yards by the crew Ted had hired. The two-by-four frames of the office, next to the big archway opening onto the side street, were upright, but that was all. Still there was a lot of room here, and both of them, without saying it, were seeing this yard as it would be someday—jammed with wagons, its long sides housing the mules and the busy blacksmith shop and spacious corral.

Ted lifted his hand and pointed and was about to speak when, out of the darkness of the stable's side, a man stepped. He had a

gun held close to his midriff and it was pointed at them. His face
was masked.

He said harshly, "Reach for it!"

Ted and Cole, taken by utter surprise, did just that. The man
stepped over, shucked their guns to the ground and then stepped
back.

"It's payday tomorrow, boys. Got anything in your safe across
the alley?"

Cole said quickly, "You're a day too soon, my friend."

Ted laughed then. "Don't bother to bluff him, Cole." To the man
he said, "We pay by check, mister. There's not a dollar in the
place."

"Seems to me I read 'bout your stealin' some money from Monarch," the man said.

"That was a lie," Ted said easily.

"Lie or not, you better get the money."

"I haven't got it, I tell you."

The man cocked his gun; the sound of it was very clear. "I said,
take me to it," he said coolly.

Cole had the sudden conviction that this man meant business.
He was sure of it when the man said, "You thought long enough.
You aim to?"

Cole said swiftly, "Sure. Come along."

And on the heel of his last word there came a sharp *crack!* from
the alley.

The robber stepped backward and glanced toward the alley gate.
There, standing in it, was a woman, her gun leveled. Celia!

"Get back, Celia!" Cole shouted.

For answer she shot again. This time the bandit swiveled his gun
around, thought better of shooting at a woman, then turned and
raced off into the darkness. Cole lunged for his own gun in the dirt,
found it and sent two shots after the man, knowing he missed him.

Then he hurried over toward Celia. Ted was there, and as Cole
came up he turned to him. "This isn't Celia," he said.

There was a deep, warm laugh from the girl, and she said,
"Would you like me to stand over by the lantern so you can see
me?"

She stepped into the yard, and the light from the lantern fell
upon her. She was smaller than Celia, and her dark hair was parted
in the middle and brushed tightly back to a knot at the base of her

neck. The full gingham dress she wore was patched but neat and clean, and there was a look of pride in her handsome face. Her dark eyes were wide-set and full of humor as she looked from one to the other.

"I'm Letty Burns," she said.

Ted and Cole swept off their hats. Ted stammered, "I never saw you before in my life, Miss Burns, but that cutthroat meant business."

Letty Burns held out a small gun in her palm for them to see. "In all the time I've been in Piute," she said, half laughing, "that's the first time I've ever used that." She put it back in her pocketbook.

"It did the trick," Ted said, smiling too. "Thing I can't understand, Miss Burns, is how you happened to be in the alley at just the right time."

"I was waiting to see you, Mr. Wallace," Letty Burns said. "I wanted to talk to you."

"Then let's go into the place," Ted said. "A stable yard is no place for that."

Celia came out of the kitchen as they entered, her face flushed and eyes filled with pleasure at seeing them. When she saw Letty she looked at Ted, and Ted introduced her to Letty, explaining their meeting. Then Letty Burns sat down and Ted pulled up a chair beside her. Cole didn't say anything.

"What was it you wanted to see me about, Miss Burns?"

Letty Burns looked at Cole, who was standing beside Celia. "It's —it's private, if you don't mind. Business."

Cole started to go out into the kitchen after Celia, but Ted said to him, "Wait," and he came back. Ted added to the girl, "We're partners, Miss Burns. If it's business you can speak to both of us."

Letty Burns's gaze faltered and she bit her lip. Then she said swiftly, "It's about a job. Oh, I know I'm a woman, but won't you listen to me?" She was talking to Ted now. "You're building a new wagon yard, I've heard. I also know that both of you are working as teamsters. But soon, when the new place is done, you'll need someone in the office—someone better than the old man down below who just sweeps out and refers business to you." She looked at Cole, whose face was expressionless.

"I've had training," she went on, talking to him now. "I can keep books, write letters and take care of all the correspondence, pay bills, make out invoices. I've done it all before. When my father was alive, before his store burned down in San Francisco, I did all the work. I can do it."

Cole looked at Ted, who was looking at him. Ted said, "Teamsters are a pretty rough crew, Miss Burns."

"I can take care of myself," Letty Burns said quickly. "Just give me the chance. I'll work for very little, and I'll prove I'm worth more than you pay me!"

Cole said quietly, "You need the work, Miss Burns?"

She swiveled her head to look at him. The way he phrased the question, the way he said it, the faint suggestion of doubt in it, the inscrutable expression in his eyes made Letty Burns study him closely. But he was only waiting, a tall, unsmiling man with a kind of sober courtesy that she shouldn't be afraid of. She said simply, "Very badly."

They didn't speak for a moment, and then Ted said to Cole, "It's something new. Lord knows, all the male brains in this man's town have quit and are working for miners' wages." He glanced at Cole, and Cole knew he liked this girl. And then there was that affair out in the stable yard which was in the back of both their minds. It was a debt to be paid off to this girl. Ted's look was questioning.

"There's no reason why a woman can't do as good bookwork as a man, I reckon," Cole said quietly, noncommittally, leaving it squarely up to Ted.

Miss Burns smiled her thanks and then looked at Ted. Ted said finally, "If you can do all you say, Miss Burns, there's no reason why you can't have the job. I'm keepin' a rough set of books in the office below. If you can get them straightened out in the few days before our new shack is up over in the yard then the job's yours." He was going to look over at Cole to see if he approved, but Letty Burns came to her feet, her face lighted with joy. "Then you'll try me anyway? I'll prove it, Mr. Wallace!"

And Ted Wallace, enchanted by her smile, never got around to glancing at Cole for his approval. For Celia came into the room then and announced supper was ready for them all, Letty Burns included.

It was a pleasant meal there in the tiny kitchen, and Celia treated Letty Burns as an old friend when she learned of Ted's decision, which she did not question. Letty was the first woman Celia had met in Piute, and they immediately began talking of

clothes and places and recipes and such, as women will. Letty
Burns had a quick wit, and more than once during the meal Ted
Wallace threw back his head and laughed. She was a resourceful
girl, for there were few ways for her kind of woman to make a
living in Piute. Cole listened, joined occasionally in the talk, and
when they were finished excused himself.

He heard Letty say to Celia, "I'm going to work a little for my
supper anyway, Celia. We'll go through those dishes in no time if
we both pitch in."

When Cole walked out of the kitchen into the living room Letty
was overriding Celia's protests, while Ted laughed at them both.

In the living room Cole stopped in front of the table. There was
Letty Burns's pocketbook on the table, and Cole gazed at it gravely
for a long moment.

Then, hearing the three of them still talking in the kitchen, he
reached over, opened it and drew out the gun. He plugged out the
shells, glanced at them and put them back.

As he slipped the gun back in the pocketbook Ted called,
"Ready to go over to the Cosmopolitan, Cole?"

"Any time," Cole replied. He reached in his shirt pocket for his
sack of tobacco, and the gesture was an absent-minded one. He was
wondering about those shells in Letty Burns's gun.

For, as he had thought when he heard her shooting at the
holdup man in the wagon yard, they were blank shells.

Harvey Girard, like most of the well-paid executives of the Piute
field, lived in the Cosmopolitan House. There was, indeed, no place
else to live in comfort, for the town was still raw and not shaken
down in five years of its growing boom. But Harvey Girard was a
working man all the same, not one of the big money men from San
Francisco. As a consequence he could not afford one of the second-
floor suites and had his room on the third floor. And the Cosmopolitan House, once it passed the second floor, forgot its elegance
and spaciousness and was just another frontier hotel. The stairs
from the lobby to the second floor were broad and carpeted; from
the second to the third floor they were narrow, steep, uncarpeted
and dark.

Climbing them, Cole and Ted went single file, and when they
reached the top of the stair well they found themselves in a dark
and narrow corridor lighted by one single lamp.

They found Girard's room and knocked and were bid enter. The room was a sitting room, littered with papers, topographical maps, books and ore samples. For the China Boy mine, whose superintendent was Harvey Girard, lay a long ride from Piute, and this was his town office. He was a big man, gruff and craggy-looking, about fifty. When he saw them he smiled faintly.

"I didn't think it would take you this long to get here," he said as he shook hands with them.

Ted grinned and said, "We came up to weep over the Monarch's hard luck."

"Don't laugh," Girard warned them good-humoredly. "I've got a hunch you'll be in the same spot."

"Well, that's what we came for," Ted said. "We're goin' to try it day after tomorrow. Ten wagons, twenty-ton load and two trips, sunrise to dark."

Girard shook his head. "I hope you make it. I really do. Because if you do then my directors will quit hounding me to get the ore moved and let me alone."

"Have you got the ore there ready to load?" Cole asked.

Girard nodded and said dryly, "The same ore I had ready to load on the Monarch wagons this mornin'—minus eighteen tons."

"Then have a crew there early day after tomorrow," Ted said, "because we'll swing it, Girard."

They talked a moment longer and then left. At the door Girard wished them good luck as they went.

Going down the hall, Cole was figuring. Day after tomorrow they would be up at three, so that they would hit the China Boy road at daybreak. The last of the wagons, working on night shift at the Lord Peter, could be left at the mill and be checked by the mill's blacksmith soon afterward. The mules would already be fed and rested. Tomorrow, then, would be the day to pick the drivers and get them ready to go.

They were at the stair well, and Cole stepped aside to let Ted go first. Ted went ahead, and Cole took the first step.

And then something rammed into Cole's back that sent him kiting into Ted, slamming into him with every ounce of his hundred and seventy-five pounds.

The force of that blow never gave them a chance to catch their balance. Cole grabbed wildly for the rail and missed. The force of Cole's impact into Ted had bowed Ted's back, and then he fell sprawling on his face down the steep steps. His momentum pinwheeled his body in a slow arc and he crashed onto the floor below with an impact that shook the stairs. And Cole, helplessly following, fell on him a moment later.

It was Cole who moved first, dragging himself to his knees, head hung, gagging for breath. Ted was lying on his face, motionless. Someone attracted by the racket had come out of a nearby room, and he and Cole reached Ted at the same time.

Cole, still half stunned from the fall, turned Ted over. Ted was unconscious, Cole saw, through a haze of pain, and then noticed that when Ted was turned his right leg lay at an awkward angle.

The stranger put it into words. "Handle him easy. His leg's broken."

8

By the time they had carried Ted over to the rooms above the office both Sheriff Linton and the doctor had arrived. Cole shooed the curious out of the room and then went back into the bedroom, where Celia was waiting while the doctor examined Ted. Sheriff Linton, always tactful, was in the kitchen conversing with Letty Burns in low tones. The doctor, a small, dry man with a professorial beard and a racking case of hiccoughs, straightened up and told Celia, "I think it's just concussion from the fall. Skull isn't fractured. *And,* of course, a broken leg." He turned to Cole. "I'll need splints." And he described them, hiccoughing as he talked.

Celia, tight-lipped and wide-eyed, looked at Cole from the other side of the cot, and there was pure misery in her eyes. There was nothing Cole could say to her, and he turned and went down into the compound, crossed the alley into the wagon yard and went over to a pile of lumber.

When he stooped to pick up the boards he felt a sudden and painful twinge in his shoulder. He had been afraid of that, and he cursed soundlessly. Since the fall his left arm had been numb, and something in the back of his mind had told him not to try and use the arm for a while. He flexed his fingers and found he could move them. It was all right then, and he went back up the stairs, his face set against the quiet, constant pain in his shoulder.

Both Celia and Cole helped the doctor set the leg, and Ted only stirred fitfully under the pain. When it was finished the doctor left, and Celia and Cole went out into the kitchen where Letty and Sheriff Linton were.

Letty Burns came over and said, "Is there anything I can do, Celia?"

Celia only smiled and said there wasn't, and Letty Burns thanked her and said good night. As she was going out she said, "I suppose you won't want me to start work tomorrow, Mr. Armin?"

"Yes," Cole said. "Good night." Letty Burns went out, leaving Sheriff Linton with them. Cole and Sheriff Linton regarded each other like two wary dogs, each remembering the other night, of Cole's escape with the money.

"I'll only take a moment," Linton said briskly. "Armin, how did Wallace happen to fall?"

"I was at the top of the stairs, and Ted was ahead of me. Somebody—I didn't see anyone or hear anybody—kicked me in the back. I slammed into Ted and we both fell down the stairs. Ted broke my fall, or I'd have a broken leg, too, I reckon."

"I see," Sheriff Linton said, considering, plucking his lower lip. "Any motive for anybody doing it?"

Cole's sober eyes held Sheriff Linton's for a long moment. "Does anyone in this man's town need a motive for committin' any crime, Sheriff?"

Sheriff Linton flushed. "There is a lawless element here, I grant you. But we do our best."

"When it suits you," Cole said quietly.

He and Sheriff Linton regarded each other carefully. There was a cold and wicked anger in Cole's gray eyes, and in the sheriff's there was a searching, resentful curiosity.

"Very well," Sheriff Linton said meagerly. "I don't do anything if you won't co-operate."

"I'll co-operate," Cole murmured. "Lord knows, it's plain enough to every man in the street by now what happened. The Monarch wanted the China Boy contract. They couldn't cut the mustard. Now we got the wagons and enough teamsters we aimed to try it. All of a sudden Wallace is shoved downstairs and his leg is broken." He didn't smile then. "By a strange coincidence, Sheriff, Ted Wallace is one of our best teamsters. Now you go on from there."

"You're implying," Sheriff Linton said, "that Monarch was interested in keeping Ted Wallace from making the try?"

"Not implyin'; I'm tellin' you."

Celia watched his face. The muscles along his jawline were standing out, and there was a kind of downbearing anger in his eye that was still under control.

"Nonsense," Sheriff Linton said in his best manner. From him this one word was the ultimate in ridicule.

"That's all, Sheriff, except one thing," Cole drawled. "Western Freight has got a job to do, and we aim to do it. But when we get that job done there's goin' to be trouble. I keep a tally book in the back of my mind. It's addin' up. Tell Monarch that."

"You'll answer for any trouble that starts then," Linton said crisply.

"Starts, hell. I'll finish it!"

Linton lounged erect, bowed stiffly to Celia and left the house. They could hear his measured footsteps as he descended the outside stairs.

Celia said then, "You've made him angry, Cole."

Cole's sultry gaze shifted to her, and slowly the anger in his gray eyes died. "I reckon," was all he said.

Celia went in to look at Ted, and Cole remained where he was, leaning against the cold stove, his eyes soberly musing. This had him baffled, this town, its law, its politics. He could understand Sheriff Linton's reluctance in refusing to handle anything as hot as the arrest of Craig Armin for stage robbery. Any sheriff anywhere would feel the same. He could also understand, though not approve, of the sheriff's glib acceptance of Craig Armin's story that the safe was blown by Ted Wallace, a logical suspect. But this tonight, the sheriff's refusal to believe any wrong of the Monarch, was the tip-off. It told Cole that he could never expect help, only hindrance, from the sheriff's office, and that in the end this would be a matter for cold steel and hot lead to settle, with Sheriff Linton against him.

And that thought placed the situation squarely before him. The Western Freight Company was now his responsibility. It was in the thick of a fight, expanding, crowding its luck, taking risks and bucking long odds—and Ted Wallace, the man who knew it and could pull it through, was flat on his back and would be for a long time. And he, Cole Armin, with no experience except an ability to read a man carefully and then act accordingly, was left to take up the reins. He couldn't even back out, for there was Celia to consider. But couldn't he? Wasn't that better than bluffing and losing in the long run?

Cole tramped slowly into Ted's bedroom. Ted was sleeping now, and Celia pulled the covers up to his shoulders. Then she leaned her back against the wall, hands behind her, and raised her glance to Cole.

"What will we do, Cole?" she asked.

Cole was ashamed of what he had come in there to say to her. He never said it. Something in Celia Wallace's face stopped him. It was the look of trust that was in her eyes, and it told him better than words that she was putting all she had in his hands. He was a humble man really, but he forgot that when he studied her.

"Do?" he echoed, and his voice was low, strong, confident. "We'll do what we aimed to do all along, Celia. Tomorrow Ted will be able to talk. He can run the business from his bed, and I'll see his orders carried out. As for the China Boy trial—well, Ted never claimed he was the best teamster in Piute, did he?"

"No," Celia said slowly.

"Then we'll hire the best. And I'll ride herd on him with a gun in his ear if I have to."

Celia laughed then, but her laugh was quavery, and Cole knew that she was close to breaking. He added, with more confidence then he felt, "You get Ted well, Celia. I'll take care of Western."

But it was two long hours after he was in bed before he slept. He stared at the ceiling, beating his brains for a way out. He knew so little about this business, so damned little! Were there other good teamsters? Could they be trusted? Would Girard back out when he found Ted was flat on his back?

A thousand questions such as these finally put him to sleep.

Sheriff Linton left the Wallaces, still smarting under Cole Armin's threat—for it was a threat. But behind his irritation was a wholehearted disgust for Keen Billings, his partner. Why had Keen risked such a fool trick as this affair in the hotel? It was clumsy and risky and it might have killed both Cole Armin and Ted Wallace, the two people most necessary to their plan.

Sheriff Linton went over to the Cosmopolitan House bar. Keen Billings wasn't there. Patiently, then, he started the round of the saloons. In half an hour he found Keen. He was playing poker in one of the back rooms of Womack's Keno Parlor. When Billings saw Linton open the door he excused himself without having to be asked and joined the sheriff in the corridor under the gallery of the saloon.

"Come out in back," Linton said brusquely.

Together they sought the alley behind the saloon. Once in the darkness and alone, Sheriff Linton turned on Billings.

"What kind of a ham-fisted play are you pulling off, Keen?" Linton asked hotly.

"Me?" Keen said just as hotly. "I was aimin' to ask you the same thing. What did it get us?"

For a moment Sheriff Linton's surprise made him speechless. Then he said, "I'm talking about shovin' Ted Wallace down the stairs."

"So am I! Why'd you do it?"

"Why did *I* do it? I didn't, you fool!"

Of one accord they moved together into the rectangle of light shining from one of the saloon's back rooms. Once there, they looked at each other carefully. There was surprise and protest on both their faces.

"Wait a minute," Linton said. "You mean to tell me you weren't up there on the third flood inside that end room? You didn't shove Armin?"

"So help me," Keen swore, "I ain't been out of that chair in there all night, Ed. Ask the boys."

"And I was at the faro table in the Cosmopolitan House when it happened," Linton said slowly. "I can prove that too."

They were speechless for a moment, and then Keen framed the question: "Then who did shove them?"

Linton shrugged, watching him. "I know one thing though. Both of them might have been killed by that fall. And where would we be if they were?" The suspicion was not wholly gone from his face.

"We'd be plumb out of luck," Keen said sulkily. There was suspicion on his face too. "You damn well better get to work on that, Linton. That come close to costin' us."

"I intend to."

There was a long pause, during which neither of them voiced his doubts of the other. They were each suspecting a double cross of some kind on the part of the other, but one thing confounded them: how could this accident help either of them?

Keen Billings spoke first, maybe because suspicion died first in him. "All right. You didn't do it, and I didn't do it. But it's done." He paused. "It comes to me, Ed, that maybe it helped us after all."

"How?"

"Ted Wallace had been to see Girard, hadn't he, about tryin' for the China Boy contract tomorrow or the day after?"

"Yes. That's what Girard said."

"And Ted's got to drive one of the teams. He's got ten wagons and maybe nine good teamsters—no more."

"Well?"

"That fall put Wallace out. He'll need another teamster."

"Then he'll get one."

"But what if he can't get one?" Keen murmured.

After a moment's pause Linton smiled and shook his head. "But there are lots of free teamsters in Piute, Keen."

"But if there ain't?"

"Then Western can't even make a try for the contract. But you can't buy every teamster off."

Keen Billings' eyes were musing. He smiled slowly and said, "Not without money, no. But Craig Armin has the money. And he'll put it up to see Western lose that contract." He waved easily. "So long, Ed."

"Where are you going?"

"I got an idea, Ed. I'll hunt you up tonight if it works." His face grew a little bit hard then. "You just do your sheriffin' and let me worry about this."

They parted there, Keen Billings heading down the alley, Sheriff Linton going into the saloon. But in the back of both their minds the seed of doubt had been placed. Could he trust his partner? And if he could, then who shoved Ted Wallace down those stairs? And that led them both to ask another question.

Was there somebody else in on this? Who was it then, and what did he want out of it?

9

Juck was sitting on the bottom step of the stairs at daylight when Cole, having already breakfasted while Ted and Celia slept, came out.

Juck was dressed in clean clothes for once, his thick chest straining the buttons on his red calico shirt. When Cole came to a halt beside him Juck said gloomily, "I heard. He's all right, ain't he?"

Cole nodded grimly. "Juck, this is up to you and me now. Girard will have the ore ready tomorrow. We've got the wagons. How many teamsters?"

Juck said promptly. "Nine. No more, with Ted out."

"But can't you find another? What about the crew on day shift?"

Juck shook his head. "We're just breakin' 'em in, Cole. Like you. They're good boys on small wagons but not for this job."

"Isn't there a teamster in town you could hire, say for a bonus for this job and a month's wages until Ted is up?"

"I dunno," Juck said skeptically. "We can sure as hell try. We got a whole day to find a good man."

"Then come on."

This early the streets of Piute held less people than at other times. Smoke lay in a thin blanket above the town, fogging the air of the cloudless desert sky, for the day shift of mines started at six and this was the smoke from breakfast fires. The stores were not open yet, but the saloons were still going and the sounds of carousing inside were just as strong and just as dreary as they had been at midnight. Only the faro barker had retired, with no more prey in sight.

Juck headed for the Desert Dust first, saying that the boys driving day shift always came in at this hour for their eye openers.

The lamps of the Desert Dust were still going, and there might have been thirty customers, all with dinner pails, lining the bar. Juck looked at the crowd critically and then bellied roughly up to the bar, poking his neighbor in the back. "Where's all the boys?" he asked him.

For answer the teamster pointed to a blackboard leaned against the backbar. On it was chalked the legend:

*All teamsters wanting work at $8.00 a
day report at Monarch offices at 3 A.M.*

Juck spelled it out slowly and then looked at Cole. Craig Armin had outsmarted them once again. Then Juck yelled to the barkeep. "Harry, how many of the boys went out with Monarch?"

"Any damn man that knowed the front end of a mule from the hind end," Harry said.

"Joe Humphries?"

"He went."

"Arch Masters?"

"Gone."

Juck called off a dozen names, and they all had gone. Finally Juck growled, "Gimme a bottle and two glasses. I got to think."

He took the bottle and glasses over to the table, and Cole sat down beside him. Cole refused a drink; Juck took two, prodded his hat off his head and stared out the window. Cole felt helpless, for this was Juck's play. Presently Juck gave him a name. Cole wrote it down. He wrote down more names, and when Juck confessed that that was all he or anybody else could think of Cole looked at the list. There were ten names.

"Mind you," Juck said, "I kin git you men who can cuss a mule. But they'd puke the first time they looked at that drop off the China Boy road. I'm talkin' about teamsters, not hired drivers for livery rigs."

They split up the list, got horses at the wagon yard and went their separate ways. Cole's way took him up to the Six Aces mine, to two boardinghouses, one of which had moved, to the back room of a barbershop, to two saloons, to a tent at the edge of town, to three gambling joints, back to a barbershop and out to the Sierra Negras stamp mill. By noon he had canceled every name off his list. Two of the men on his list had taken the Monarch offer; one was sick; one had moved over the mountains, and the other had picked up a job on the California run the night before. Still it wasn't hopeless, for Juck had his half the list.

Cole rode into the wagon yard at one o'clock and dismounted. He was hungry and he was anxious about Ted. But more than either he hated to face Celia until he knew about the extra teamster.

It was half an hour before Juck rode in and slipped off his horse. Cole could tell his luck by the expression on his face, which was somber. Juck shook his head as Cole ceased talking with Phil Grimes, the hostler, and came over. "How about you?" Juck asked.

"None."

Juck swore bitterly, and Phil Grimes, coming up behind them, said, "You hunted up that list of relief drivers Ted has?" The whole crew was worried now and didn't have to be told what was amiss.

"Where are they?" Cole asked.

"In the office somewheres."

Cole crossed to the rear door of the office and went in, Juck behind him. At the desk, which was almost the only furniture in the long room besides a couple of straight-backed chairs, was Letty Burns. Cole started with surprise at the sight of her, and Letty looked up from her ledger.

"I got to work like you told me, Mr. Armin."

"Fine. Fine," Cole said absently. He had forgotten her. "Have you looked through the stuff?"

"No sir. I found the books, though I had to look through a lot of papers."

"Did you find anything that looked like a list of names? Of relief teamsters?"

Letty Burns frowned and shook her head, then stood up and invited them to look. The task was hopeless besides being foolish. Ted would know where they were, but to see Ted he had to face Celia, and he shrank from that. He stood there, undecided, when Letty Burns said quietly, "You're looking for a teamster to replace Mr. Wallace?"

Cole nodded, glancing at her.

"Have you tried old Jim Rough?" she asked.

Juck snapped his fingers and boomed, "That's one we missed, Cole!"

"Can he do it?"

"Hell, yes! He's half Piute and old as sin, but he can still throw his weight around on the end of a brake strap. He put this road in

here from Californy, and he could freight a ship in here usin' pi-
anos for wheels." He headed for the door. "Sit tight, Cole. I'll git
him." And he vanished.

Cole felt a great relief flood over him. He sat down, and Letty
Burns said, "May I go out for lunch now, Mr. Armin?"

Cole grinned. "Go ahead." He watched her clear her desk and
pick up her pocketbook. It was the same pocketbook she carried
last night, and it put him in mind of something.

"Tell me," he said. "How'd you happen to know about this Jim
Rough?"

Letty faced him, her pretty face unreadable. "Didn't I tell you
last night that my brother freighted here for a while? I've heard
him talk of teamsters—the best ones. I—well, I just remembered."

Cole nodded. "If it works it saves our necks."

Letty smiled. "I hope I can prove to you and Mr. Wallace I'm
worth my pay."

Cole watched her go out, and he doubted if they had made a
mistake. But only time would tell.

Letty stepped out onto the jammed sidewalk and let the crowd
push her two blocks. When she came to Miller's Emporium she
turned in. The store was crowded, so that no clerks bothered her
immediately.

Slowly she drifted down past the dry-goods counter, past the
grocery counter and to the hardware counter, which was near the
door.

A big crockery churn stood by the door that let out onto the
loading platform, and she pretended to examine it. When everyone
was busy she slipped out the back door, went leisurely down the
steps and headed across the cinders to the shed on the alley. She
rounded the corner of it, and Keen Billings, who was hunkered
down in its shade, came to his feet. He touched his hat politely, but
there was eagerness in his eyes.

"It worked," Letty said briefly. "Juck has gone out to see Jim
Rough now. I'm quite sure they didn't find another man, because
they came in looking for Ted Wallace's list of relief teamsters."

"Good," Keen said, and a smile broke his heavy face. "Nice
work, Letty."

"You're sure nothing bad will happen over this?"

"What could?" Keen Billings said, spreading his hands and

shrugging. "They just won't have enough drivers. They'll see that and quit."

Letty Burns watched him closely, and then her glance shifted to the cinders of the alley. She said slowly, "Ted Wallace's broken leg came just at the right time for Monarch, didn't it? He was pushed, you know," and she looked up at Keen.

"I was wonderin' when you'd come to that," Keen said steadily. "I'll swear on anything you want that I didn't do that, Letty. More than that, I'll swear that I don't know who did."

His eyes were steady as Letty watched them.

"I can remember what happened to Pete when he had a broken leg," Billings said solemnly—and shrewdly. "I don't like to see men die that way."

Letty winced.

"I didn't shove Ted Wallace. But that's no sign I don't aim to take advantage of his broken leg," Billings said frankly. "I do. Is there anything wrong with that?"

"No," Letty said slowly. "I suppose not."

"You're not forgettin' Pete, are you, Letty?" Billings went on. "It took him a long time to die. And Ted Wallace isn't even goin' to die. He's just goin' to wind up broke, that's all." He added with gentle irony, "Or are you agin' our doin' that, seein' as he killed your brother?"

"No," Letty said huskily. "No, I don't object! I want to help!"

"Good. I'll see you day after tomorrow right here." He looked shrewdly at Letty, knew he could hold her forever and walked away, very careful to tip his hat before he left her. Ladies—real ladies—were funny about little things like that, Keen knew.

10

Cole was awakened by a hand on his shoulder. He came awake with a rush to find Celia, a gray flannel wrapper held about her and her golden hair cascading around her shoulders, standing by his cot. The flush of sleep was still in her cheeks.

"What are you doin' up?" Cole whispered severely.

"You don't need to whisper," Ted said from the other cot. "I haven't slept a wink all night. I'll bet Seely hasn't either."

"I haven't slept much," Celia confessed. "But I wasn't going to lie in bed and let you get your own breakfast again, Cole. Now hurry up and dress while I make breakfast. It's two-thirty."

She left the room, and Cole began to dress. Ted watched him from the bed, his eyes alert with excitement. Suddenly he said, "I'd give a thousand dollars to see that today, Cole. And I'd give two thousand to drive one of the wagons."

Cole, pulling on his boots, grinned faintly. "You're lucky. After it's over I'll likely have gray hair—just watchin' it."

"Tell Juck to watch that shale. If she starts to go tell him to jump and the hell with the wagons."

"I told him yesterday—twice," Cole said.

Ted grinned and said, "All right, old-timer, rib me. But you don't have to stay in bed here in Piute until it's over."

Cole stood up and walked over to the bed. He mussed Ted's hair and said, "Go to sleep. When you wake up we'll have a contract from the China Boy that will cure your leg in a day."

"Beat it," Ted growled.

Celia sat opposite Cole at breakfast, a cup of coffee before her. She had never looked lovelier, Cole thought, what with the excitement of this day before her. She wasn't afraid; she was confident, and somehow, against his will, some of her confidence was communicated to him. She asked him again about Jim Rough, and Cole told her all he knew.

"He must be good," Cole finished. "He was cranky about his wagon. Said he wanted to look it over last night and made us leave it at his shack. He looked tough as rawhide. Old but tough."

"Then we'll do it, Cole!" Celia said. "I know those other men. They're rough and they drink and fight and carouse, but they're loyal. They like Ted—and they like you too. Juck would die for you!"

Cole flushed and looked down at his plate. "Maybe he's goin' to have to," Cole said dryly.

Celia laughed then. "You hate a compliment, don't you, Cole?"

"I never got one," Cole said slowly.

"Then you'll get one now," Celia said. "Last night when Ted was hurt I saw the doubt in your eyes. You didn't know if you were good enough or knew enough to run Western Freight. You've felt all along that you shouldn't be here. But rather than show me that, you bluffed it through." She smiled, almost shyly. "Thanks for that, Cole. I'm all right now. I know we can pull through, but it was a bad minute."

Cole looked briefly at her, his face a deep red, and then at his plate, and when that didn't help he came to his feet.

"I've scared you," Celia said, laughing a little.

Cole suddenly smiled and shook his head. His tongue was serious. "Not scared me the way you think, Celia," he said slowly. "You scare me a little, I reckon, by what you expect of me."

He dodged out then, stopped in Ted's room long enough to say good-by and then clattered down the steps. When he looked back Celia was standing in the doorway, a candle in her hand. She waved at him, and he waved back, disturbed and restless and uneasy.

But the sight of the wagon yard across the alley changed all that. By the light of several lanterns the nine picked teamsters were just finishing their hitching. There were five wagons here. Four more were out at the Union Milling, and one was at Jim Rough's house, a mean little shack out on the flats below town on the way to the China Boy road. Phil Grimes, the hostler, and a couple of boys had already left with the remuda of mules, which would make up the teams for the other five wagons.

When Cole walked into the circle of lantern light where the teamsters were gathered, listening to Juck, they greeted him with friendly equality. They liked this tall new boss of theirs. He asked them questions that made sense, and he didn't give orders to them like they were one of their mules. He had savvy and he didn't talk much, and there was something in his eyes behind their friendliness that warned a man to speak softly.

"Line 'em out, boys, if you're ready," Cole said. "Juck, you and me will head for Jim Rough's place."

Cole saddled his horse, mounted and swung out ahead of Juck's wagon and led the clanking, jolting parade out of town. The mules, rested for a day and grained well during their rest, were feeling salty. A lantern, swung from the collar of a lead mule of each wagon, lighted the night and gave an eerie appearance to the procession. It looked to Cole as he looked back over the line as if this might be a funeral procession of five giants.

Presently, when they reached the turnoff to Jim Rough's place, Cole left the mill road. The reason he had asked Juck to come along was that Juck could give Jim Rough, who had never been to the China Boy, some rough pointers on the road.

Juck's lantern cut off toward him, and the others went on ahead. A moment later Cole could see another lantern in Jim Rough's yard. That would be Phil Grimes, dropped out with Jim's mules and helping to harness.

When he came closer he saw that the teams were hitched to the wagon, pointing toward the mill road. As he approached Phil walked toward him, and Cole pulled up.

"Come in here and take a look," Phil said grimly.

Cole slipped from his saddle, feeling a sudden uneasiness. He followed his hostler into the house and looked where he pointed. On the bunk lay Jim Rough, snoring deeply, and at the foot of his dirty bunk was an overturned jug. The reek of whisky was rank in the room.

"I throwed some water on him, a hull bucket!" Phil snarled. "He's out cold!"

Dimly Cole heard Juck pull up in the yard outside. He stepped over to the bunk and knelt by Jim Rough and slapped his face sharply. The man did not move, although his snoring stopped. He had been a big man once, but now his flesh was shrinking. His face had a kind of debauched content when in repose, and a sudden rage shook Cole.

He hauled the teamster to a sitting position and belted his face with his hand. Jim Rough's head rolled loosely and did not raise.

And then Juck's voice broke the silence. It was the most blistering cursing Cole had even heard. Juck strode over to the bunk, took Jim Rough from Cole's hands, stood him on his feet and shook him until Cole was sure his head would snap. When Juck let him go Jim sagged to the floor like an empty sack.

Juck raised his glance to Cole, dread in his eyes. "Well, by God!" he said bitterly. "That licks us!"

"Can you do it with nine wagons, Juck?"

Juck only shook his head. "No chance. Not and move four hundred tons."

"And there isn't a driver you can get, any kind of a driver?"

Again Juck shook his head. "Not one that wouldn't wreck his outfit."

For one still moment, while the hostler whispered bitter curses, Cole looked at Jim Rough. The ability that lay somewhere in the brain and muscles of this sodden flesh shut them away from success. He was a sorry-looking thing, wet and drooling and already snoring again, and everything in Cole protested at the sight. A stubborn anger was lighted inside him, and it burned slowly as he beheld this wreck of a man. He thought of Ted Wallace and Celia. A man, seventy years old, tough and burned out and useless, had licked Ted and Celia. And here he, Cole Armin, stood—young and just as tough and not burned out. Cole came to a sudden decision then.

He looked up at Juck and said quietly, "Juck, I'll take his wagon."

Juck didn't say anything for a moment. He was weighing all the odds against the man, and it was his observation that brains and guts made up for a lot of experience that was lacking. A little luck was all they needed, and this man was lucky.

"That's the way to play it," Juck said matter-of-factly, and his big mouth broke into a grin. "We can't waste no time." And he started for the door.

By sunup they were on the long, steep haul to the China Boy. Cole was second in line, behind Juck, and he was trying to remember the things Juck had told him to watch out for. Instead he was remembering the scene at the foot of the grade when he, instead of Jim Rough, had come up with the tenth wagon past the other wagons lined out waiting for them. Juck had been ahead of him, and as Juck came abreast the others he passed the word about Jim Rough.

And as Cole came along after him it was the way his men looked at him that made a difference. To a man they grinned at him or waved at him, wishing him luck. They liked him. They wanted him to do it, although nobody but Juck really believed he could. That helped, and he wished savagely that he knew a tenth as much about this business as his men did.

He returned to his study of the road, which he saw through the dust haze that Juck's mules were kicking up. In the wagon behind him he could hear tough little Bill Gurney, not a care on his mind, whistling in an off key. Cole concentrated on the road.

It was deceptively mild at first, not half so bad as the road to the

Glory Hole. But soon the switchbacks started to tighten up and the grade increase. The rocks, almost barren of growth except stubborn dwarf cedars in the cracks, still held yesterday's heat, and as the sun climbed they started to warm up again. Slacked loosely in the saddle of the near mule, Cole studied each curve, each straight stretch, each grade. He tried to forget what lay beyond the road. Sometimes it was just a sheer drop on one side that fell to dim, hot canyons below. Other times it was the same sheer drop on both sides as the road, having worked up to the maximum height on this ground, crossed on a narrow ridge of rock to start a new climb all over again. And as the road climbed higher it got narrower, and then finally, swinging downgrade onto a narrow neck of rock that divided two deep canyons and coming around the ample curve beyond it, Cole saw a change in the character and color of the rock in the straight stretch before him. He didn't have to be told what it was. This was the shale that all the teamsters feared.

The whole gray side of this mountain was shale, and the road had been gouged out of it, following each contour. Above and below him the shale stretched out like tiny slate shingles on a vast roof. It was a treacherous footing at the best of times, for this was not living rock; it was a great shabby scale, feet deep, on the steep shoulder of the mountain. It slid and buckled at the first touch of frost. It could be surprisingly solid at times; other times, when the whole mountain was deserted, the men at the China Boy beyond would hear it start to move. A great dusty avalanche would roar for an hour, and when it was over the road was gone. Like some savage beast, bent on a cruel whimsey, it was unpredictable and strange. Men feared it and rightly. Teamsters hated it. And putting twenty tons of ore and twelve tons of mules on its face at once was flying in the face of Providence. This, then, was what Western Freight was fighting.

The China Boy mine lay at the head of a canyon a mile beyond the shale. Like its sister mines it seemed to cling precariously to the side of the mountain, its heap of tailings lying in a great smear down the face of the canyon.

In reality, however, it lay on a flat, the cluster of buildings backed against the mountain. There were barracks here, for this was too far to travel to work from Piute. There was the candle house, the grading shed and enginehouse and the office buildings. The huge grading shed had been perched on the edge of the can-

yon, and the tailing used to shore up a road under the rear of it.
The wagons could drive around under the rear of the shed, be
loaded by gravity in a matter of minutes and be on their way down
through this high desolation to the flats.

Girard was there to meet them, and there was little time wasted
in talk. The mine was working steadily, its sign the regular chuff-
chuff of the hoist engine. Skips from deep in the earth rode to the
surface, were dumped in ore cars pulled by mules and tracked over
to the grading shed. Juck drove his wagon under the loading chute,
and while it was being filled he talked to the teamsters gathered
around him in the pitilessly hot sun. They were a rough-looking
crew, dusty and unshaven and utterly sober.

"Keep the order you got, boys. Stay far enough apart so's you
can see through the dust. Remember you're overloaded and ride
that brake. If she gets away from you, jump, and the hell with the
outfit. That's all."

The men scattered silently to their teams, and Cole walked up to
his with Juck. Juck wanted to speak but was reluctant to do so.
Finally he blurted out, "You remember that, Cole, about if it gets
away from you. Nothin's worth havin' twenty tons of ore piled on
top you—not even this damn contract."

They were at Cole's wagon now. He said quietly, "I'll watch
you, Juck. And don't loaf on account of me."

"Right," Juck said gloomily. "Another thing. When you're
drivin' over them bad rocky places keep your right leg out of the
stirrup and your eye on the tongue. She'll swing around and break
your leg quicker 'n you can wink." And he strode off, a man of
little sentiment.

Cole smiled to himself. In Juck's mind he was almost as good as
dead. But not quite, and that was what counted.

Once loaded, Juck drove off and Cole drove under the loading
hopper. He and the loader didn't talk. The shovel men distributed
the load; he drove ahead to fill the tandem wagon, and when that
was done he was ready.

Then the mules were under way down the road toward the shale.
Cole had his right hand on the brake strap buckled to the saddle
horn, his other hand holding the reins of the swing team and resting on the jerk line for the signal to the lead team. He tested the
brakes now and knew then by the pressure exerted that this was a

tremendous load. He looked back at the curved brake lever, thick as his arm, and wondered if it was strong enough. It had to be.

After that he was in a tight and busy little world of his own. All he could see were the humping backs of his ten spans of working mules and the dim shadow of Juck's wagon ahead of him in the dust. A man had to remember just three things, he kept telling himself: the signals on the jerk line, which would turn his lead team left or right; the driving of the swing team, just ahead of the leaders; and the brake. The brake was what counted.

When he saw Juck hit the shale nothing happened, and he breathed deeply once more. He was braking gently now, keeping the sullen, lurching load behind him under control.

He had a bad moment when he hit the shale too. It crunched and cracked under the broad wheels of the wagon, but there was no other sound. He couldn't hear it anyway if it started to slide, and that was some comfort. He didn't need to worry.

Presently he was through the shale safely and now saw the dip to the curve below. The road swung down sharply into an abrupt but banked curve and then vanished from sight around the shoulder of the mountain. He pulled his brake strap and the dry squall of the brakes keened out over the rataplan of the mules' hooves. This would be the test of the braking, Cole thought behind thought and leaned more heavily on the strap. The squall turned into a wail.

And then there was a sharp crack, the rending of wood, and the strap slackened suddenly.

The brake lever had snapped! He didn't need to look; he knew!

For one slow second the wagons didn't react, and then the rumble of their wheels increased. And in that one second Cole knew he had a choice to make. There was this drop to the curve. By luck and the grace of God he might make the turn, and beyond that was a fairly long stretch, and beyond that he couldn't remember.

Either jump and get clear, or stick and try and bull it through.

He found his chest contracted, and suddenly he yelled at the mules and cursed them in a wild and savage passion. He'd made his choice. He'd stick and risk it!

The mules, roused out of their drowse by the urgency in his voice, stepped up, and the wagon fell into the downgrade. He didn't need to signal the leaders. There was only one way for them to go. What he must remember, he told himself, was not to cut the swing team too short, or the top-heavy wagons would roll over and off the cliff.

And now the mules were in a run, and the curve started. The ponderous wagons behind lurched and rumbled, like some great monster working up its anger. The lead team and the following team were around the curve now, skipping the chain as it swung in close to the shoulder. Then the third, four, fifth and sixth spans went out of sight, and the low chain screamed as it rubbed the rock shoulder. The seventh and eighth spans of mules veered away from it in panic and then got jerked around the bend. And now the ninth, the swing team, was set for the turn. With an iron hand Cole drove them to the very lip of the drop and then turned them gently on the edge of that wicked curve. The near mule almost went off, and in his panic he lunged into his collar and fought.

Cole knew how close that was, because his mule was on the lip of the drop for three full seconds and he could look down into that abyss.

And now, in this second, he would either win or die. He didn't look back. He yelled at the mules, running now, and they lunged into their collars. The heavy chain whipped back with a snap into a straight line, knocking number-three team's feet from under it. The other mules reared and dodged and skipped as the chain swung back under them. But the swing team pulled!

There was a slow groaning sound from the wagons behind as they took the curve. They skidded, and Cole could hear the scream of their iron tires on the rock. He wouldn't look back! He could only wait.

And since nothing happened in those two seconds and the mules were still running he knew that the wagons, running at a tremendous speed now, had taken the curve upright.

Ahead of him was a fairly long stretch of straight road that barely sloped, and then it turned imperceptibly to the left, and the mountain fell away. This was the narrow ridge between the low shoulder and the one they were on now. It was a long curve over that narrow ridge, but beyond was the up pull, which would stop the wagons. The off mule of number three was crippled, but he was still on his feet, panic driving him.

Would the wagon pile into the mules on that ridge, or could they keep ahead of it? Cole didn't know. But he did know that once they were across the ridge the mules would fight and rear and buck and could not be made to pull the load. Without brakes it would settle backward then, gain momentum; the tandem wagon would cut short; the tongue would break, the other wagon would knock it over, and everything—the wagon, the mules and himself—would be dragged off the edge and into the chasm below. He would have to block the wagons to stop them rolling back. But how? And he had to get across the ridge first.

He yelled at the mules again now, for the thundering wagons were creeping up on them. For one brief moment there was nothing he could do. And in that time he reached down for the brake strap and pulled it up to him. First the strap, and then the severed brake lever that had been trailing under the wagon. There was nine feet of it left—good strong oak. He laid it awkwardly across the saddle and unbuckled the brake strap from the horn. The wagons behind him howled and jolted, but he would not look at them.

The lead mules swung into the ridge, cutting short. The others, the second, third, fourth and fifth, took it at a dead run too. The chain began to crowd the near mules off the edge, but the ones on the sixth and seventh teams did the impossible feat of straddling it. If the turn had been more abrupt they would have been swept off their feet.

And then, forcing the swing team to hug the inside edge, Cole swung into it. The wagons rocked and jolted and drove, their wheels close to the edge, but they turned that imperceptible bit that was needed to cross the ridge.

And then suddenly they were on the upgrade. The lead mules took up the slack and then the others; and at the pressure on their collars they started to fight and pitch. The wagon slowed down and Cole freed his feet from the stirrups, the brake lever still in his hands. Now the mules weren't pulling at all, and abruptly the wagons slowed to a stop.

Cole vaulted out of the saddle onto the lip of the road and let the front wagon coast to a stop beside him, the panicked mules forgotten. And as the big rear wheels of the wagon ceased moving Cole rammed the brake lever in between the spokes of both wheels, up against the bottom of the wagon bed, and then stepped away, watching, praying.

The wagons settled back. Cole watched the spokes. There was a muffled crack as the thick spokes took up the tremendous weight.

For one terrible second Cole thought they would snap, but then they ceased moving. The brake lever bit into the spokes. He could see it take up all that tremendous weight and bite deeper and deeper, quarter inch by quarter inch. The spokes cracked again, and then all was still with the wagons. They had stopped moving backward; they were blocked!

Cole put his hand on the wagon side for support and looked up toward the mules. There was Juck, and his wild voice was lifting in the kind of curses the mules understood. Team by team, he quieted them, fighting his way back to Cole.

Cole sat down on the edge of the road, his knees suddenly weak. He hung his head in his arms and stared at the dust.

He heard Juck beside him say in a low voice, "Goddlemighty, boy. You done it!" And Juck put a rough hand on his shoulder and bawled, "You done it, you hear? You done it!"

Cole came to his feet, his hands shaking, and looked at Juck. Juck's face was wet with sweat.

"I seen it all," Juck said. "I watched you die, Cole! I had you dead and smashed like a tomater three times. Three damn times!"

Cole smiled and shook his head. "I might's well die right now, Juck. I used up all the luck a man has in a lifetime."

"What happened? The brake lever break?"

For answer Cole pointed to it. He saw Juck stiffen and he looked at the lever, the butt end of which stuck through the spokes.

And there, for anyone to see, was the freshly cut mark of a saw. The brake lever had been sawed almost in half, so that when it was applied in a pinch it would snap.

Cole and Juck walked up to it and stood looking at it. There was a smear of candlewax and ashes along the outside. Whoever had done it had disguised the cut nicely to harmonize with the weathered gray color of the oak.

Juck said after a long, long pause in a mild voice, so calm that it was final, "I'm goin' to tear the heart out of Keen Billings for that, Cole."

"No, you aren't," Cole said in a quiet and terrible voice. He looked off at the curve he had rounded only minutes before. The third wagon, driven by Bill Gurney, was just inching around it. "No, Juck," he said quietly. "He's mine. If you kill him, I'll kill

you. He's mine, and so is Craig Armin." He looked at Juck, and
Juck only nodded, understanding.

They turned to the repairing of the brake lever as soon as they
had examined the now-quiet mules. The off mule of the third span
had a deep cut in its leg where the chain had struck, but it was not
crippled. For a brake lever for Cole's wagon they used a spare
timber Bill Gurney always carried for such an emergency.

Afterward, ready to go again, Juck went on to his wagons. Cole
whipped up his own team while Bill pulled the block, and they
were off again.

At six o'clock that night, after the last load of China Boy ore
was in the Union Milling hoppers, Cole had a contract in his
pocket from Girard, who had ridden down behind them on their
second and uneventful trip. But it was a different Cole Armin who
told his teamsters that their score at any saloon in town that night
would be on Western Freight. It was a different Cole Armin who
grinned at their cheers, who accepted their awkward congratulations for a feat that they would never have had the guts to try and
that made him their superior to them.

And it was a different Cole Armin who stood beside Juck as the
men scattered for their wagons. The old Cole Armin would have
been content in his quiet way, knowing that he had done a good job
well.

But that wasn't what he was thinking. There was a hard core of
hatred in him now, and a man could see it in the bleak coldness of
his gray eyes. His face was haggard, dusty, but his eyes were burning. Juck saw it. He said awkwardly, "Mebbe we better go tell
Ted."

"You go, Juck," Cole said. "I've got some business to do.
Alone."

Juck shifted his feet. "Alone?"

"Alone." He gave Juck the contract and walked off.

11

Letty Burns lived in two rooms of an unpainted frame house on a side street west of the town's center. The other half of the house was owned by a hoistman at the Jeffers and Beecham mine who worked nights, and his wife kept the same hours. But in spite of the fact that there was apt to be noise on the other side of the house to keep her awake Letty Burns preferred it to the steady roar of the nighttime riots inevitable had she chosen a place closer to town.

It wasn't strange, then, that she mistook the knock on her door when it wakened her for the movements of the family next door. She turned over and was about to go to sleep when the knock came again. She heard it this time, and a little flicker of fear washed through her. She was jumpy lately, she thought. She got out of bed, put on her wrap and called, "In a moment, please."

She lighted the lamp, and her fingers that held the match were trembling. Putting the lamp out on the table, she threw the covers over the bed, then crossed the sparsely furnished room to the door. A gun was lying on the table beside the lamp, and, remembering it, she came back for it. At the door she called, "Who is it?"

"Cole Armin."

Letty unlocked the door and stood aside, and Cole Armin came in. He had to stoop a little to clear the low door, and when he stepped in Letty saw his boots, his corduroy pants and his cotton shirt were powdered with dust. She drew her wrap around her, brushed her black hair out of her eyes and said in a friendly voice, "I heard about it, Mr. Armin. Congratulations."

"Thanks," Cole said wearily. He didn't apologize for coming. He walked over to the table, laid his hat on it and watched Letty close the door.

"Do you want me for some night work, Mr. Armin?" she asked.

"No, Letty. Sit down," Cole said mildly. When he looked at her his eyes were smoky and uncomfortably piercing. Letty settled on a bench against the wall, well out of the light, and said, "Then you

Track Down And Capture Exciting Western Adventure!

WANTED!

LOUIS L'AMOUR COLLECTION!

REWARD OFFERED

Mail your "WANTED" poster today. (see inside)

Make your "wanted" claim and receive your rightful reward!

• A free authentic Louis L'Amour calendar!

• A free preview of the bestselling SACKETT

And much more…

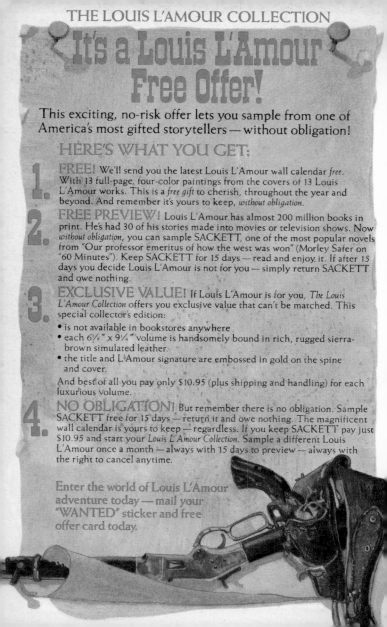

Track down and capture exciting western adventure from one of America's foremost novelists!

• It's free! • No obligation! • Exclusive value!

might as well sit down too. Would you like me to make some coffee?"

Cole only shook his head and settled into the rocker. He put his elbows on his knees and clasped his hands before him and stared at the floor. Letty was suddenly uncomfortable at his strange actions. For one brief instant she knew stark fear, and she fought it.

Cole said, looking up, "How much of what went on up there at the China Boy did you hear, Letty?"

"Just that we moved four hundred tons before the deadline and that Girard gave you the contract. Why?"

Cole didn't answer. He looked at his boots again and then began to talk in a mild voice. "Letty, I'm going to kill a man, two men—maybe three. But I want to be sure first."

Letty didn't speak for a moment. "Sure of what?" she said in a small voice.

"Of their guilt." Cole kept looking at her. "Today, with twenty tons of ore at my back, the brake lever on my wagon broke."

"Your wagon?" Letty said swiftly. "I didn't know you were driving one, Mr. Armin."

"I had to. Jim Rough was drunk—hog drunk—when we went to pick him up this morning."

"Oh." Letty's mouth stayed half open as her mind took all this in. She hadn't talked to Billings today. She knew that Jim Rough's condition hadn't stopped Western, but she hadn't heard what had happened. It all came to her now, and she understood. Cole Armin had driven instead of Jim Rough. And the brake lever on his wagon had broken. Letty shivered a little and licked her lips. "I see," she said in a faint voice, then she corrected herself. "No, I don't, entirely. Your brake lever broke."

"It was sawed half in two," Cole said, still watching her. "It was done last night, either by Jim Rough or by somebody who got Jim drunk and then did it. Jim has gone."

"How horrible," Letty murmured. "You—you weren't hurt?"

"I'm here," Cole said. "That don't matter." He straightened in his chair and leaned back, stroking his chin with the palm of his hands and keeping his steady gaze on Letty. He didn't speak, and Letty dreaded what was coming next.

To forestall it she pretended ignorance. "I'm afraid I don't follow you, Mr. Armin. What do you want?"

"I got to thinkin' how queer all this was," Cole murmured. "Ted

Wallace is shoved downstairs and his leg broke. We can't hire a relief driver because they've all been paid by Craig Armin to get out of town. We're up a stump." His voice changed. It was gentle now. "You savvy that much, Letty?"

"Yes."

Cole went on. "We're up this stump when all of a sudden you pull a name out of the hat. Jim Rough. He's free to work; he wants to." His voice died, and he kept looking at Letty.

Letty knew it was here and that she couldn't pretend ignorance any longer. Her face was red, too, she felt. "I see," she said quietly. "It does look bad for me, doesn't it?"

Cole didn't say anything. Letty couldn't look at him, and yet she had to defend herself. The panic within her drove the words out of her mouth. "I didn't recommend Jim Rough, Mr. Armin! I asked you if you'd seen him. Juck recommended him; I didn't!"

Cole still didn't say anything. Letty mistook it for doubt and, smart girl that she was, she decided to force her hand. She came erect and walked over to the table. Her anger looked genuine, and she was pretty as she spoke angrily to Cole. "What right have you to say that, Mr. Armin? What proof have you that——"

"Proof of what?" Cole said quickly.

Letty stopped, hesitating. "Why—that I knew anything about the brake lever being sawed."

"I didn't say you did," Cole drawled, his face impassive. "I said I just wondered."

"What right have you to wonder then?" Letty asked hotly.

Cole rose, walked over to the bench where Letty's small gun was lying. He picked it up, glanced at her; then, seeing the heavy, iron-framed mirror on the opposite wall, he raised the gun and shot at the mirror. The mirror was untouched. He tossed the gun on the bench, then leaned against the wall and looked at Letty.

Her face was a study. There was fear, panic, courage and defiance in it for a few seconds, and then it broke into a lovely smile. She laughed then, a laugh that was not quite steady.

"I see. You're a very observant boss, Mr. Armin."

"I got good ears," Cole drawled.

"That holdup was faked. I admit it. What would you do to get a job if nobody would give you one? You'd make one for yourself, wouldn't you? How? By putting someone in your debt if you could. That's what I did. I knew if I seemed to have saved you from a robbery then you'd be in my debt. When I asked for the job it would be harder for you to refuse. It was, wasn't it?"

"I reckon," Cole said slowly. He was still looking at her, but a little of Letty's courage had returned.

"It was crude, I know. I paid one of these toughs to hold you up. I can't shoot very well, so I used blanks. And you heard the difference between the shots. But I got the job, and I can hold it, Mr. Armin. Because I did that does that give you any right to accuse me of plotting your death?"

Cole didn't say anything.

"I was starving, Mr. Armin. I *had* to have a job! It was either that or the honky-tonks. Should I have chosen them? Who was hurt by my trick? Anybody? No. As for Jim Rough, I told you how I happened to know him. I know a lot of good freighters—Arch Masters, Joe Humphries, Zeke Bothwell, Lute Hamlin. I can't vouch for their characters. I couldn't vouch for Jim's."

"I see," Cole said.

"You believe me?"

Cole came over to the table then and picked up his hat.

"Do you?" Letty insisted.

"Letty," Cole said, raising his glance to hers, "I'll tell you the truth. I don't know. I'll tell you some more truth. If I ever doubt you again then it's the last time I'll ever have to." He hesitated a moment, his piercing gaze on her, then said quietly, "I can take a tinhorn because he's born that way. Or a thief because he needs somethin'. Or a coward, Letty, because he can't help it. But a traitor, no. Good night."

"Wait, Mr. Armin!" Letty said desperately. "I'll do any-thing——"

A call from out in the street broke off her speech. She listened. There it was again, and it was plain.

"Fire! Fire! Everybody out!"

Cole opened the door. Off toward the center of the town the sky was lighted up. The unwritten frontier law which made every man help his neighbor was sometimes broken by men, but the call to help at a fire was a command that everyone obeyed. Cole turned to Letty and said, "You're still workin' for Western, Letty. Good night."

When Cole had gone Letty's knees gave way and she sank down

in the chair. That was close. And behind her fright was stark fear. Was she in a compact to kill Cole Armin and Ted Wallace?

As soon as Keen Billings heard about Western landing the China Boy contract and the accident that had happened to Cole Armin's wagon his spine went cold. He got the news in late evening, for it had taken time to work upstreet from the Desert Dust, where it was fast becoming one of the teamsters' legends. Keen heard it at the bar of the Aces Up saloon. He left his drink untouched, sought the street and headed for the Cosmopolitan House.

He found Sheriff Ed Linton at a faro table in the ornate gambling room beyond the bar. Keen had to take off his hat and stifle his excitement as he tramped across the thick rug through the crowd of well-dressed men to the table where Sheriff Linton was sitting.

Keen said politely, "Business, Sheriff. Can you step outside?"

Sheriff Linton excused himself in a low voice, pocketed his chips and followed Keen through the saloon and into a deserted corner of the lobby. Keen faced Sheriff Linton, and there was fear mixed with his anger.

"Your double cross didn't work!" he snarled in a low voice. "He's alive, and the word is he's on the prod!"

"Man," Sheriff Linton drawled, "what are you talkin' about?"

"About Cole Armin!" Billings said harshly. "He's out to nail up my hide!"

"But why should he be?" Linton asked blankly.

"Listen, Ed. Don't stall. I know damn well you sneaked back to Jim Rough's last night after we left and sawed that brake lever. I tell you, he come through it!"

Linton shook his head blankly, then hauled himself up. "Start from the beginning. This doesn't make sense. I take it the Western tried it with nine drivers?"

"Haven't you heard, damn you?" Billings snarled. "They got the contract, moved four hundred tons of ore with ten wagons! Cole Armin drove Jim Rough's wagon. On one of them grades he pulled on his brake lever and it snapped off. He come out of it, the Lord only knows how, without crackin' up and goin' overside. And that brake lever was sawed half in two!"

"I see," Linton said slowly. "And you think I sneaked back after we got Jim Rough drunk and sawed it?"

"Didn't you?"

"I staggered home and fell asleep with my clothes on!" Linton said harshly. "I was so drunk I couldn't have held a saw, and you know it!"

"So was I!" Billings countered hotly. "You carried me part of the way!"

And then again there was that stalemate. And Keen Billings shivered a little. It was funny, but he had the impression of some invisible person standing there listening to what they were saying.

"Then you didn't saw that brake lever?" he asked hollowly.

"Man, I couldn't have!"

"And I didn't. Then who did?"

They stared at each other, half suspicious, half puzzled. Keen Billings said finally, "Ed, someone is out to kill Cole Armin, and right now! And Cole Armin thinks it's me! He's goin' to make a try for me and damn quick! And I can't get him first, or how do we frame Craig Armin?"

Linton, wide-eyed, shook his head in blank inability to answer him. "First Ted Wallace gets shoved downstairs. That was meant to kill him. Then that brake lever is sawed, aiming to kill Cole Armin. Keen, if I ever told the truth in my life I'm tellin' it now. And I want it from you too. Did you shove Ted Wallace or saw that brake lever?"

"And put a noose around my own throat?" Billings countered. "No! Hell, no, I didn't!"

"Then who did?" they both asked each other.

At that moment a man ran into the lobby and yelled, "Fire! Fire! All out! The Monarch's on fire!"

12

Keen Billings moved first. He lunged for the door, yelling over his shoulder to Sheriff Linton, "Get Craig!" Then he was in the middle of the street, running down it with the scores of men who were pouring out of the saloons and gambling halls in answer to the emergency call.

When he reached the Monarch wagon yard he saw that the feed barn and the blacksmith shop, on the east side of the yard, were in flames, great pillars of fire and billowing white smoke lifting to the sky above them and lighting up the whole yard and surrounding street. The Piute Volunteer Fire Department was already there with the pump wagon, and they had two hoses run into the Monarch well. Another hose reached to the rear of a saddle shop across the street. The firemen were already working frantically over the hand pumps, dousing the roofs of the adjoining stables.

Quickly, then, Billings organized a crew to lead the panic-stricken mules out of the stables. While he was working two bucket brigades were formed to assist the firemen. The wagon yard was cleared of spectators, and the others settled down to the grim business of keeping the fire under control. Wisely the barn and shop were given up as lost, and the effort of the fire fighters was turned toward preventing the fire from spreading.

Into the madhouse of shouting men Craig Armin and Sheriff Linton walked. Billings, who had seen to the safety of the mules and as many wagons as the men could reach, could do nothing more now. Wiping his face with a huge bandana, he walked over to Craig Armin and Linton.

Craig Armin said nothing as he came up, only watched the fire. Linton glanced at him quizzically, but Keen Billings was waiting for Armin to say something. But Armin didn't. With his immaculate clothes, his graying hair, his erect carriage and his unreadable face a man would not have known that it was his property that was being destroyed. More than ever Billings hated his cold, contained guts.

And Keen had an uneasy feeling within him, as if sooner or later Armin was going to blame him for this too. Keen started away to check up on the activity, glad to be out of Armin's sight. He was looking at the bucket brigade, watching it work, when suddenly he hauled up and stared.

There, hat on the ground beside him, passing buckets as fast as they were given him, was Cole Armin.

For one brief moment Billings was stunned. Then his presence of mind returned. He wheeled to face Ed Linton and pointed a finger at Cole.

"There's the man that started the fire, Sheriff! Arrest him!" he shouted.

In a few moments Billings' wild shouting and cursing had drawn a crowd around himself and Cole, who had given over his place in the brigade to another man.

Sheriff Linton finally succeeded in elbowing his way through the crowd, followed by Craig Armin. Cole Armin was facing Billings, calmly wiping the sweat from his forehead with the sleeve of his shirt. His face was rock-hard, his eyes dancing with wicked lights as he watched Billings.

"There's your man!" Billings said grimly to Linton.

Craig Armin spoke then. "A magnificent bluff," he remarked quietly. "It won't work, though, Cole."

Cole Armin's level gaze switched to him, and he didn't speak. Then he looked back at Billings. "I thought I'd find you here, Billings. I've wanted to talk with you."

The tone of his voice led Sheriff Linton to say immediately, "None of that, Armin. Stick to business."

Cole dragged his gaze from Billings and said, "What business?"

"The business of this fire you started!" Craig Armin said in cold fury.

The instinct of self-preservation was strong in Keen Billings at that moment. He read in Cole Armin's face the will to plain murder, and it scared him. But now Keen saw what he was going to do, and he made one supreme effort to be casual. He had to be if he was going to get Cole Armin in jail, where he couldn't kill him.

"Your story has got to be good," Keen said grimly. "For the past hour I been listenin' to everyone tell me that you're out to get me, Armin. I was waitin' for you. But you didn't have the guts to back up your brag, did you? You figured you'd fire the Monarch instead."

Cole's hands fisted at his sides, and muscles in his arms tensed till they ached. There was a wild light in his eyes for a moment, and then he settled back on his heels. Keen Billings knew then that he had him.

"What are you waitin' for, Sheriff?" Keen said. "There he is."

Cole spoke slowly. "There's a matter of an alibi, Sheriff. I wouldn't make an arrest just yet."

"Your friends will lie for you," Billings sneered. "That's to be expected."

Linton said, "Let's hear your alibi."

"I don't aim to bother with one if you don't aim to believe it," Cole drawled softly. He was counting on the crowd helping him, and there were murmurs of, "Give him a chance, Sheriff."

But Sheriff Linton wanted to know how far it was safe to go, and he said, "I'm givin' you your chance, man, before I make the arrest. What's your alibi?"

"I was with a lady," Cole said quietly.

There was a guffaw from the crowd that was quickly throttled as Linton raised a hand for silence.

He shook his head. "I'm afraid Celia Wallace's word is prejudiced, Armin. It's got to be better than that."

"It is better than that," Cole murmured. "I didn't say Celia Wallace."

"Then who?" Billings blurted out.

Cole's eyes were watchful as he said, "Letty Burns."

Keen Billings knew immediately that he must not look at Linton. None of them must give this away by so much as a move. But a hot elation pounded through his veins as he stood there, making his face unreadable. He knew Craig Armin wouldn't have given it away by so much as the wink of an eyelid, and he wanted Craig Armin to speak.

Craig did. "I don't believe I know the lady," he said shrewdly.

"You'll meet her," Cole drawled. "That is, you will if you decide to listen to her. If you won't then what's the sense of seein' her?"

A man in the crowd volunteered, "She ain't lyin' for no man, Letty ain't."

Keen suppressed a smile and looked at Linton. Letty might not lie for just any man, but she would for Monarch—for them. Cole Armin had walked into the neatest trap possible. In ten minutes he would be in jail on an arson charge, and Linton could keep him there forever.

Linton saw this, too, but he did not show it. Craig Armin wasn't aware that Linton knew Billings had hired Letty Burns. He mustn't give it away to Craig. Nor to Cole. He must pretend blank ignorance, although he thought that maybe—just maybe—Letty, in this pinch, would not help Cole Armin. He said, "All right. Let's see this Letty Burns then."

Cole wheeled and walked to the gate. Linton fell in beside him. Keen Billings fell in alongside Craig Armin. Not a word passed between the four of them as they walked the two blocks to Letty Burns's place. Billings nudged Craig Armin, and Craig Armin raised a finger to his lips. Billings nodded and his face was impassive. They would let Cole walk into the neatest frame-up ever devised for a man.

At Letty's house the sheriff took charge. He knocked, answered her question and was the first through the door when she opened it. Letty looked alarmed, Keen saw, but that was to be expected when four men walked into her bedroom.

"You're Miss Burns?" Sheriff Linton asked.

"Yes."

Keen hadn't told Letty of his association with Sheriff Linton, but that wouldn't matter. He wished she wouldn't look at him so questioningly.

Sheriff Linton went on carefully, "There was a fire tonight at the Monarch yard. Circumstances point to Cole Armin. We believe he set the fire." He paused. "He says he was with you when the fire started and long before. Was he?"

There it was. The statement had been framed so as to give Letty no doubt as to what they wanted her to answer. Keen was aware that Cole Armin was watching him closely, not Letty. And that made it impossible for him to signal her. But she didn't need a signal anyway. She was a smart girl and understood things.

Letty's face was dead white. She opened her mouth to speak, closed it, licked her lips and then said in a voice just above a whisper, "Why—yes. He was with me."

Keen Billings could gladly have killed Letty Burns then. He barely controlled a wild impulse to hit her.

Cole Armin was smiling faintly. He said, "Good night, gentlemen."

The three of them stood there, confounded. But it was Sheriff Linton, a cynical man who had anticipated Letty's answer and provided for it, who took over then.

"Not good night," he said smoothly to Cole. "Nothing of the kind, Armin."

Cole said gently, "Remember your promise, Sheriff. You gave it in front of several dozen people—and they elect you."

"Let me finish," Linton said, a trace of a smile under his fine silken mustache. "What I was going to say is that it isn't good night—yet. You've made threats against the lives of the Monarch operators. They have already complained to me." He looked at Craig Armin, who nodded.

"I think," Linton said slowly, "I'll have you put under a peace bond, Armin. You've threatened murder. I'll advise the judge to set the bond at five thousand dollars."

Before Cole could answer Juck's booming voice came from the door: "Go ahead, Cole. I'll git the money from Ted and beat you all to the sheriff's office."

He stood there in the door, a gun in his fist, a smile on his broad and ugly face, out of breath and still dirty and a little drunk to boot. But he was there, solid as a log.

He said to Cole, "I figured you didn't mean it when you said 'alone' back there."

13

It was an hour before Celia, led by Juck, stepped into the dirty office that held Cole, a bored justice of the peace, and Sheriff Linton. Celia looked harried but not at all frightened, and Cole knew Juck had told her of this business. She had a shawl around her shoulders, and a lock of her golden hair straggled down over her forehead, displaced by her contact with the jostling half-drunken crowd that lived on the streets of Piute after dark.

Cole came to his feet at her entrance, and she walked straight to the sheriff's desk, put the canvas sack of money on it and then turned to Cole.

"I'm sorry I took so long, Cole. I had to rouse Mr. Shay at the bank and show him the China Boy contract before he would take Ted's note." She looked at Sheriff Linton, angry contempt in her green eyes. "I'm sure you'll find the amount right."

Linton bowed and waved to the J. P. In silence the J. P. made out the peace bond and the papers were signed.

When he was finished Sheriff Linton said dryly: "If you want that five thousand dollars back, Armin, you'll keep out of trouble. One more of your ruckuses in this man's town and you'll wind up behind bars. And the county will spend your five thousand convictin' you too. So walk softly, mister."

Cole said quietly, "I'll walk softly, Sheriff, but I aim to make some mighty big tracks in the next few days. Keep an eye out for 'em."

"Is that a threat?" Linton asked, smiling.

"You figure it out. You'll have to sooner or later."

He took Celia's arm and they stepped out onto the sidewalk. There were a thousand questions Celia wanted to ask him, for she had not seen Cole since early that morning when the men started out for the China Boy. She was bewildered by all that had happened, scarcely knowing whether to be happy over the contract or disheartened over the loss of the money. But one look at Cole's face as he guided her across the street told her that this was not the time for talk.

At the far sidewalk Cole said, "Juck, take Celia home and then come back to the Desert Dust." And he touched his hat to her and walked off into the sidewalk crowd.

He would have given a thousand dollars at that moment to be alone where he could think. But all around him was the swarm of miners and the boomtown trash. He walked among them, deaf to their talk, his head hung, his eyes musing. There were a lot of questions that needed answering, but there was one that needed immediate attention. If he hadn't set fire to the Monarch then who had? It was only by the thin margin of Letty Burns's alibi that he was a free man and not a jailed one this minute. That fire had been set to jail him. It almost had.

It was foolish to suppose that Keen Billings had set it, for his anger was genuine. And no man would risk setting a whole town ablaze just to get another man in jail. Besides, it was he, Cole Armin, who was after vengeance and not Keen Billings. His forehead beaded with sweat as he thought what he might have done two hours ago. He was out to murder a man then, after he was satisfied with the proof. The fire had saved him. The anger wasn't gone, but with it was mixed a little wisdom that had been forced on him by the peace bond. He smiled bitterly at that. He was like a fly who has blundered into a spider's web that held him by one thin thread, and he could read his fate. Thread by thread, he was being trapped, made impotent. Soon he would be worse than useless to Western Freight. Already tonight he had cost the company five thousand dollars which it could not afford. He wondered bleakly if it would sink them.

He shook these thoughts off as he came to the corner saloon on the side street where the Desert Dust was located. He put his shoulder against the wall there and waited for Juck, and his thoughts were somber. He must take this thing apart piece by piece. And the first thing would be to find out who set that fire.

Juck came along presently, and Cole swung in beside him without a word. The Desert Dust was a howling, brawling bedlam, and when Cole came in his own teamsters let out a yell for him that could be heard for two blocks. He drank a round with them for courtesy's sake, and then Juck beat on the bar top for silence.

"Quit drinkin' a minute and listen!" Juck bawled.

Cole's eight teamsters, to a man, were around him, and they sobered at Juck's announcement, eying Cole.

Cole prodded his hat back off his forehead and grinned at them. "Damned if I know how to start," he began. "I'm comin' to you boys for help." He waited until they had nodded and bid him go on. "You heard about the Monarch fire tonight. Some of you saw it."

"Pity the hull damn thing didn't go," little Bill Gurney said.

"I got blamed for that," Cole said, and the men fell silent. The rest of the barroom did, too, for the other teamsters were listening.

"I got blamed for it," Cole repeated, "and I got out of it by the skin of my teeth. I also got put under a peace bond by Sheriff Linton. If I draw a gun, except in self-defense, I'm in jail, boys."

There was a murmur of protest that soon died.

Cole said slowly, "I'm goin' to make you boys a proposition. Maybe I'm wrong, I dunno. But here it is." He paused, eying them. "If the man who set that Monarch fire will admit it I'll guarantee to get him out of town ahead of the sheriff, pay his fare to the Coast and give him a hundred dollars besides."

His offer fell on complete silence. His teamsters looked at each other and then at the other teamsters. The silence ran on and on until Bill Gurney finally said, "How come you want to know, Cole?"

"I've got to know," Cole said quietly, "because if that man stays in this outfit he'll get me hanged."

Bill said slowly, "Why?"

"Because Sheriff Linton is watchin' me. I answer for everything that happens to the Monarch. I got to play 'em close to the chest, Bill. Monarch will move against us again. I dunno how, but they will. And this man—the man who set the fire—won't trust me to keep you boys safe. He wants to get even by himself." Cole grinned. "I don't blame him. Still I don't aim to hang for what he does to them." He looked around at the eight faces that ringed him. "Understand, I'm not blamin' this man. He could have drawn Jim Rough's wagon just like I could. And a man is goin' to fight over somethin' like that or he ain't a man. But still he's gettin' me hung—inch by inch. Anybody want to talk?"

There was utter silence. Cole let it run on for a moment, then he said, "I reckon not. All right. I got one favor to ask of you boys."

"She's yours," Bill Gurney said.

"If you got any bright ideas that will wreck Monarch come to me with 'em before you try it." And Cole smiled.

The men laughed at that. Cole set up a round on the house, told the barkeep to send him the bill in the morning and went out alone. On the street he felt anything but festive. He was baffled, discouraged. He had a deep conviction that these men liked him and that they were loyal. They trusted him. If one of them were guilty he would have come forward, taken Cole's offer and headed for the Coast on a bat. But since none of them spoke up the question was still unanswered. Who set the Monarch fire? He hated to face what he was going to have to face when he saw Ted and Celia.

When he reached the house he trudged up the stairs, his step weary. Celia was waiting for him in the living room, and Cole took off his hat and said hello. "How's Ted?"

"He's awake, waiting for you," Celia said soberly.

Ted's long face did not smile as Cole walked into the room. "Sit down and talk," he said gloomily. "And hurry, dammit!"

Cole sank to the cot. He tried to work up a smile, but it didn't come off. He began with finding Jim Rough drunk, mentioned that a sawed brake lever had almost wrecked them and went on.

"Your brake lever, you mean," Ted interrupted brusquely. "Juck told us."

Then Cole told about the fire, how Billings had accused him and how Letty Burns gave him his alibi. Ted knew about the peace bond, and after that Cole confessed his inability to discover from the teamsters who set the fire. He was sure Ted would worry about that. Instead Ted said as casually as possible, "So Letty Burns gave you your alibi?" and looked at Cole. "It was lucky you were there on business, wasn't it?"

"That's right," Cole said. He felt Celia looking at him too, and he knew they were waiting for him to explain his presence at Letty's. But he couldn't. He was ashamed of suspecting her loyalty, and while it was done in anger it would sound shabby and small if he confessed it now. Besides, in the back of his mind he wasn't wholly sure of her yet. And if he told them of his suspicions now and they were proven untrue later he would never forgive himself. So he stubbornly said nothing, and Ted's glance, curious and almost resentful, fell away from him. Cole looked at his hands and said wryly, "Well, it looks like I've jinxed the outfit for fair, Ted."

"Why? You got the China Boy contract, didn't you?" But Ted's enthusiasm sounded hollow. What he'd left unsaid was that five thousand dollars of desperately needed capital was tied up in Cole's peace bond.

Cole said it for him, and his tone was bitter. "I did. Still I took half of it away by goin' to that fire."

Celia said loyally, "You were trying to help, Cole."

Cole shook his head. "That don't make it any better, Celia," he said wearily. "We need to buy wagons with the China Boy money —light wagons that we can use in place of the big ones that the China Boy takes. We can't get as many as we need now—and I'm to blame. And there's another thing too." He glanced at Ted and Ted looked away.

"I'm under peace bond," Cole said stubbornly. "When a man hits me I can't hit back—or you lose the five thousand and I go to jail. We're walkin' a tightrope. If nobody pushes me we'll make it. But you can be sure Monarch won't pass that up. And we can't fight back."

For a moment none of them spoke. Pared down to the bare bones, that was the situation, and they all knew it. The new yard was half finished. They had expanded too fast, and now they were caught. There was a chance that they could pull through, but only a small one.

Cole stood up and blurted out bitterly. "I'm no damn use to you now! I've been bullin' around here not knowin' what to do, and I've got you into this jam. I'm hog-tied now, and Western is, too, through me!"

He brushed past Celia and went out into the living room. He

picked up his hat and made for the door. When he tried to close it behind him he felt Celia tugging on the other side. He let go the knob, and she stepped out onto the landing beside him.

"Cole, are you going to leave us?" she asked in a quiet voice.

"No," Cole answered tonelessly. "I might's well play out the string."

"But there's the China Boy contract!" Celia cried. "It's money enough. We'll pull through some way! And maybe Monarch is scared by this fire if they believe some of our men set it! Maybe they'll let us alone." She put a hand on Cole's arm. "Isn't it worth a try, Cole?"

"I reckon," he said.

Celia laughed shakily. "You've pulled us through by hook or crook so far, Cole—you alone. You aren't going to give up now?"

Cole said in a low, bitter voice, "How can I go in there every day and face Ted and him helpless on his back? He'd know how to play it. He'd know how to swing it, how to keep out of trouble, how to lick them if he was on his feet. Me, I don't!"

"Cole," Celia said calmly, "you mustn't mind Ted. He was shouting with joy when he heard you swung the contract. But when Juck told him about the peace bond he was sunk in gloom. Tomorrow he'll be out of it and all right again. But he's grouchy and restless and discontented now."

Cole said, "With me, Celia. I could see it in his face."

"It wasn't all disappointment, Cole. Don't you know what it was?"

"No."

"It was Letty Burns."

Cole tried to see her face in the dark, and he couldn't. "Letty Burns?" he echoed blankly.

"He's in love with her, Cole. He doesn't know it himself. When Ted learned from Juck that Letty told the sheriff you had been with her tonight Ted was angry—and hurt. It's just that he's jealous, Cole. He—he thinks you were courting her while he was in bed."

"So that's it?" Cole said. He smiled in the dark, but Celia couldn't see that.

Celia said, "If you went in and told him your business with her, Cole, he'd be all right again."

Cole didn't say anything, knowing there was nothing to say. More than ever, now that he knew Ted loved Letty Burns, he couldn't tell him that his suspicions of Letty were responsible for his call. Better to let him remain jealous than tell the truth.

His silence had been long, and now he said, "I better not, Celia."

Celia moved beside him. "I'm sorry, Cole. I—I've made a terrible mistake!" she said, her voice tight and choked with shame. "I didn't know you were courting her. I honestly didn't know!"

"But——"

"Don't make it worse, Cole. I'm terribly sorry! Pretend I never said it." Her voice was firmer now, but somewhere despair had crept into it. Cole didn't hear that, though, as Celia said, "But you'll stay, Cole?"

"If you want me to."

Celia said in a small voice, "I do," and went into the house.

Cole stood there, cursing to himself, looking out into the wagon yard. He had piled blunder on blunder until now, in addition to all the rest of this misery, Celia thought he was in love with Letty. For a long and bitter moment he regretted his promise to stay. Why didn't he get out and leave them?

And then he knew he couldn't and he wouldn't. His mouth a grim line, he went back into the house to face heartbreak.

14

Breakfast next morning was awkward. Cole ate swiftly and went over to the new wagon yard. Ted was silent and did not want to talk. The whole air of the house was intolerable to Celia. It was an air of gloom and defeat, of polite suspicion and resentment and jealousy. She knew that because she shared it. For Celia was not fooling herself any longer now that it wasn't necessary.

She loved Cole Armin, and he didn't love her. Those were plain, bitter facts. He was courting Letty Burns. Hadn't he gone to Letty with the news of the China Boy contract rather than to her? Celia was a proud girl, but she was honest with herself too. Cole didn't love her and never would. For a while she had fooled herself into believing that she was why Cole was here, why he was helping them and risking his life for them. But last night, when she had blunderingly trapped him into a situation where he couldn't deny he was courting Letty, had shown her different. He was here because their gratitude over the return of the stolen money had forced him into the partnership. She remembered his reluctance that night, and she blushed. No, she and Ted had done nothing for him. He carried the burden, while they sat helplessly by and watched him fight.

Celia came to a sudden decision then. She went into the living room, straightened her hair, put on her hat and went into Ted's room. He was staring gloomily out the window.

"I'm going shopping," she said. "I won't be long."

She bent and swiftly kissed him on the forehead, and he smiled wanly at her and patted her hand. There was nothing they could tell each other, and Celia left.

But she didn't go shopping. She crossed the street and went up the sidewalk to the Cosmopolitan House. At the desk she asked for Mr. Craig Armin's room number and was given it. At suite 2-B she was let in by the Chinese servant, who led her through a short corridor into Craig Armin's elegant study.

When she stepped into the room Craig Armin looked up from his desk. He came slowly to his feet, amazement plain on his face.

"Mr. Armin, I'm Celia Wallace, Ted Wallace's sister," Celia said.

"I know," Craig Armin said, then remembering himself, gestured politely to a chair. "Won't you sit down?"

Celia wouldn't let herself be awed with the richness of the room nor the prepossessing manner of Armin. She sat down opposite the desk, and Armin sank into his chair.

Celia smiled and began: "Mr. Armin, let's forget each other's names for a moment and be human beings. Will you?"

Armin said obliquely, coldly, "I'm willing to listen to you, Miss Wallace."

"I have a suggestion to make," Celia said stubbornly. "Both the Monarch and the Western are bent on destroying each other. Surely you can see what that means?"

"I'm afraid I can't."

"Why—that nobody will win! We'll both be bankrupt!"

"And you have a cure for that, Miss Wallace?" Armin asked, smiling faintly.

"I have. It's very simple, too."

"What is it?"

"There are twenty-odd mines in the Piute field," Celia said steadily. "Why can't we divide them up—half to Monarch, half to Western?"

For once Craig Armin was speechless. His impulse was to snarl a refusal at this girl, but something in her cool and direct manner told him he would come off the worse if he abused her. He shook his head and said, "I'm afraid that's impossible."

"You mean, you like seeing men killed?" Celia countered.

Her level gaze disconcerted him. He pulled the lobe of his ear and wondered how to frame an answer. He knew he was blushing, and he hated himself for it. More than anything else he did not want to let a Wallace know that his steely surface could be cracked. When he realized he was pulling his ear and blushing, like a schoolboy caught in the jam pot, he lowered his hand quickly and composed his face.

"Miss Wallace, I don't like violence any more than you do. But I have no choice."

"But you're the one who is using violence," Celia said calmly.

"I don't want to contradict you, but the facts speak differently. Perhaps"—and he smiled faintly, inclining his head—"you didn't hear that an attempt was made last night to burn Monarch."

"That wasn't any of our doing!" Celia said hotly.

Craig Armin raised both hands, smiled and shook his head. "I'm afraid you've been spared some brutal truths by your brother and my nephew, Miss Wallace. That's all I can say."

"Then you refuse to be reasonable?"

"If being reasonable means letting another outfit steal and burn and fight their way into my business, I do."

Celia stood up. The barefaced gall of this man angered her, and she could understand Cole Armin losing his temper so easily. She was losing hers, and she didn't care.

"Very well," she said. "I can tell you one thing, though, Mr. Armin! Cole has been pushed too far already. He's not a man for guns, but he will take to them soon."

"You forget the peace bond, Miss Wallace."

"It's you who forget it!" Celia said hotly. "You forget that when Cole breaks his bond you'll be dead!"

She whirled, her skirts billowing out, and left the room, her back straight as a gun barrel. Out in the corridor she leaned weakly against the wall and put her hands to her eyes. She had lost her temper and made threats and for what? Craig Armin was inside, laughing at her. She went down the stairs, thoroughly chastened. This thing that had been set in motion was not as easy to stop as all that. For the first time she had got a glimpse of the implacable hatred of Craig Armin, and it was ugly.

When she returned home the first thing she saw on the table was Letty Burns's hat.

Ted called to her the moment the door slammed. "Celia, come in here!" His voice was angry.

When she went in Letty Burns was seated in a chair, her handkerchief to her eyes, sobbing quietly. Ted's face was dark with wrath, and his eyes fairly sparkled. Celia looked from one to the other and said, "For heaven's sake, what's the matter?"

"Just listen to this," Ted said in a thick voice. "We wondered why Cole was at Letty's last night. Well, Letty told me. Cole accused her of putting us onto Jim Rough and knowing about the brake lever being sawed. He accused her of plotting to kill him and ruining Western!"

With the contrariness of a woman Celia felt her heart lift in joy. Then Cole hadn't been courting Letty! And he had been afraid to confess for fear they would take it just the way Ted was taking it now. To cover the joy in her face Celia knelt by Letty and took her in her arms.

"My dear, my dear, don't cry. We're your friends. Cole made a mistake, that's all."

"B-but he believed it!" Letty sobbed. "Maybe he still does, when I could have betrayed him to them last night!"

"He doesn't!" Celia said. "I'm sure he doesn't. He didn't tell us."

"Th-that's why I came over to see you," Letty stammered. "I didn't want you to think that of me."

"I'd break his neck if he ever said that!" Ted said vehemently. He watched Letty, his eyes filled with pity.

Celia hushed Letty and stopped her crying. And soon, reassured, Letty left for the office downstairs. Her act had been partly desperation and partly the desire to forestall being named as a traitor. For Letty had been scared last night—scared half out of her wits. She had taken Craig Armin's cold cursing without flinching after Cole and the others left. But she was afraid of him, afraid of his threats. This was his advice, this bold stroke of denial, and much as Letty loathed herself she feared him more. For she knew Craig Armin, with Keen Billings' knowledge, was building her up for a more crucial test, a more brutal betrayal. And there was nothing she could do except go along with them now. She was in it up to her neck.

When Celia left Letty at the door she came back into Ted's room.

"Think of it," Ted said bitterly. "Suspecting that innocent girl. Why, damn him, I'll have it out with him over this!"

Celia said sharply, "Ted!"

He looked up at her, startled by the tone of her voice.

"You won't say a word to Cole about this! Do you hear me! Not a word!"

"But he can't do that!" Ted said vehemently. "It's—it's not fair!"

Celia said swiftly, "All right, it's not. Cole made a mistake. But he's helped us. He's stuck with us! He's done the best he can! If he suspected Letty it was to protect you, Ted. And me." There was that hard edge of determination in her voice that Ted seldom heard and then only when her mind was made up. "Grant a man his mistakes, Ted. We've all made worse ones than that, and you know it!"

Ted's face was torn between the dregs of anger and a new indecision.

And then Celia played her trump card, played it quietly. "If you bring that up, Ted, I'll take the next stage to San Francisco and home."

It was the least thing she could do for Cole, to spare him this. For she knew that he would leave them if Ted confronted him with this. And Celia didn't even want to think of that. She wouldn't.

Ted grinned suddenly. "Why, Seely, I guess you mean it. No, I won't say anything if you say so. But I don't like it."

Cole didn't go back to the rooms for his noon meal. That morning at the bank he had borrowed up to the hilt on the face of what was left of the China Boy contract, and the sum had been less than he hoped for. He wanted to spare Ted that news until tonight, after he had made the deal for the new wagons. For, with luck, he might strike a deal that would compensate for the other bad news.

He ate alone, in a small restaurant on the main street. And he sat alone at the counter, a tall, booted man wearing worn corduroys, scuffed half boots, checked gingham shirt open at the collar—and no gun. For this was the task he had set himself—to stay out of trouble. And real trouble was always backed with guns.

He ate slowly, half heartedly, pausing to stare at his food now and then, so that the waitress wondered at him. The thing that was gnawing at the back of his mind and had been all morning was the same question that troubled him last night. Who set the Monarch fire? He had it reasoned out that he could stay out of trouble if he had to; he could even take it when the Monarch retaliated for the fire. But what he could neither predict nor fight when it happened was another incident like last night. What if somebody spooked a span of Monarch's mules up on one of the high mountain roads and the teams and the wagon and driver went over? Sheriff Linton would pick him up five minutes after the news was broken, and no alibi could save him. He was at the mercy of the man who set the Monarch fire. The thought of it made him jumpy. Each time somebody came in the café, slamming the door behind him, Cole would jump and wait for Sheriff Linton's hand on his shoulder.

Finally, when he could stand it no longer, he paid his check and went out onto the street. A week of this waiting would kill a man, and for one desperate moment he listened to the small voice that told him to clear out while he could. He fought it down, but he couldn't fight down the conviction that he was bucking something that would lick him in the end. He was in a hole! He could only fight blindly.

The Acme Freighting wagon yard was at the far end of the main street. Once upon a time, and not so long since, Acme had been Monarch's opposition. That was before Ted Wallace came to Piute with his single wagon and his ambition. And now Acme was a monument to Craig Armin's rapacity. Cole remembered Craig Armin at their first meeting boasting of destroying Acme, and he smiled thinly at the memory. At present Acme was a small affair, with no contracts, few wagons and many debts. They kept going by hauling odd loads for the swarm of prospectors up in the Sierra Negras who were grateful to make a week's wages from an occasional load of ore.

The arch into the Acme yard was weathered and faded, and there was a look of dilapidation about the whole affair. Cole swung into the yard, saw a group of men by an empty wagon fronting the sagging stables, and he cut across to them.

At sight of him the teamsters parted—to reveal Keen Billings in violent conversation with a man in a black suit.

Cole heard Keen say, "Money is money, dammit. There's your proposition!"

"Not any price to you, coyotes," the man in the suit said grimly. "Now get the hell out of here, Billings!"

The man's eyes shifted to his teamsters, and then he saw Cole, who was in the circle of grinning teamsters. Evidently the man recognized Cole, for he smiled and nodded and then said to Billings, "I've got some business to talk over, Billings, as soon as you drag it."

Billings, scenting something, wheeled, and he saw Cole. For a second he just stared balefully at him, his heavy-jowled face petulant and still flushed by his blustering.

"So," he observed, leaning back against the wagon, "you boys have ganged up already, I see." He turned his head toward the man he had been talking to. "I'll make a flat proposition. I'll give you fifty bucks each more than the top price that Western offers for your wagons!"

"I'll burn 'em first," the man said promptly.

Cole murmured, "Your little game of freeze-out won't work, eh, Keen?"

While Keen Billings cursed him the teamsters laughed. Cole smiled, too, and Billings' face was ugly with anger. He lounged away from the wagon and said, "Don't start any trouble, Armin. I'm warnin' you."

Cole's smile died. He said, "I don't want any trouble with you, Billings. Get out."

Billings suddenly laughed. "I don't reckon I will," he said. "I'd like to rawhide you into a fight, Armin, and watch you land in jail for breakin' your peace bond. What does it take to make you fight?"

"Nothin' you got on the books," Cole answered, grinning.

Billings tentatively cursed him. Cole shook his head. "It'll take more than that, Keen. I saw my mother's marriage license."

The teamsters guffawed at that, and Billings started in again to curse. When he was finished Cole was still grinning.

Billings glared at the laughing teamsters then and swung around to Cole. He sized him up, decided to take a chance and then said, "But Celia Wallace ain't got one yet, has she?"

The teamsters' laughter died off and they looked at Cole. His smile was gone. "Be plain," he drawled. "Celia Wallace isn't married."

"But she damn well ought to——"

Cole hit him then. He knocked him sprawling in the dust against the wagon wheel, and the smack of his knuckle-studded fist on Keen's jaw could be heard all over the lot. The blow was unthinking, automatic, instantaneous. And Cole knew, behind his anger, that this was a mistake—the worst mistake he could make. But it was done now.

Keen scrambled off his back, grabbing for the gun in his holster. A teamster put his hand on Keen's wrist, pinned it to the ground, grabbed his gun and threw it over the wagon.

Keen came to his feet and backed up, fear in his small pig eyes. Cole came slowly toward him, and Keen backed into the wagon. He was terrified now, for his baiting had succeeded with a vengeance. He was hemmed in on all sides by the teamsters. And then his eyes fell on the soft oiled blacksnake whip that a teamster had left on the step of the freight wagon.

He grabbed it and in one down-sweeping gesture uncoiled it at his feet. The teamsters scattered like a covey of quail, and only Cole remained.

Billings' fright was gone now, and he laughed deep in his bull chest.

"You want to know what I said?" he asked Cole. "I said Celia Wallace needs a marriage license, mister. She come over to Craig Armin this mornin' tryin' to beg us off on account of you. And if that don't mean she's——"

Cole lunged for him. Billings brought the whip around and down in a whistle that ended in a crack like a rifleshot. Cole put up his elbow to shield his face, but the lash curled around his head and cut into his cheek. And still he ran. The lash missed him on the second blow, but the weight of the whip came down across his shoulder like a club. And then Keen Billings was cornered against the wagon, with no room to swing his whip. He brought the whip-stock down like an ax across Cole's back just a moment before Cole's head rammed into his midriff and they went sprawling in the dust.

Terror gave Billings an added strength. He grappled with Cole and they rolled over and over, slugging futilely. Billings tried to bring his knee up in Cole's groin, but Cole twisted and put his hand under Billings' jaw and shoved. Billings' head went back and he gagged and then his hold broke, and Cole rolled free. Keen made a dive for the whip. Cole lunged for him, swinging a low hook that caught Keen on the cheek and deflected his course. When he got to his feet Cole was standing on the whip.

Cole came in then, and again Billings was crowded against the wagon. Cole pinned him with one hand and slugged with the other, beating his soft face back until his head banged against the wagon side. Billings slugged blindly and kicked and cried out, but Cole fought with the cold fury of murder. When Billings, licked already, started to topple over Cole stood him erect again and slugged three savage blows into his face before Billings sat down.

"Nuff!" Billings shouted.

"Oh, no, it's not." Cole panted. He picked up the whip, flipped it out and then lashed out with it. The lash snapped and a great fresh welt bloomed across Billings' face.

Billings yelled, put his hands up and lunged unsteadily to his feet.

"Run for the gate, Keen," Cole said in a thick voice.

Billings started. Cole lashed out again, and Billings' shirt suddenly came off his back. He stumbled and fell, sobbing in his throat, fought to his feet and ran again. Cole's next blow tripped him, taking away part of Billings' trouser leg and rolling him in the dust. He scrambled to his feet again, running drunkenly for the gate. And the crack! crack! crack! of Cole's whip—seven times in all—laid a great bloody cross on his back and livid stripes across his belly before he reached the gate.

Cole let him have one more vicious lash. It curled out and wrapped around Billings' thick chest, and he cried out and fell on his face in the dust. This time he did not get up. He lay there, sobbing in the dust, his fingers clawing at the ground.

Cole leaned over him, grabbed him by the hair and yanked his head back.

"Celia Wallace isn't married, Keen. Tell me that."

"No. A fine girl—a fine girl—a——" His voice dribbled off into silence, and he collapsed.

Cole stood over him, panting, his fists wet and dark with blood.

Then he looked up at the teamsters around him, his eyes slowly fading back into sanity.

"Well, I reckon that does it," he said calmly, dropping the whip. "I might's well go to jail."

The man in the black suit commanded crisply, "Swing those gates shut, boys, and come here."

The gates were swung shut on Keen Billings, still lying in the dust. The man in the black suit came over to Cole and put out his hand.

"I'd swap fifteen years of my life for the privilege of watchin' that, Armin. I'm proud to shake your hand."

Cole shook his hand, and then the man said, "Listen careful, boys. Gather close." When the teamsters had crowded up he explained: "Cole Armin is on peace bond. When this fight gets nosed about Linton will pick him up, jail him, and he'll lose his bond. Are we goin' to let him do it?"

"No!" the teamsters shouted.

The man turned to Cole. "You get the hell home," he said. He peeled off his coat and threw it in the dust. "Mark, tear my shirt. Joe, go smear that whip handle with blood again and give it to me. The rest of you boys back up my story. When I wouldn't sell Billings the wagons he went for me. I give him the whuppin' of his life. And nine witnesses to prove it! Are you backin' me, boys?"

They were and they made it plain. Then the man—whose name Cole did not even know—turned to him and said, "Them wagons is yours for your own price, Armin. Now git out of here and keep your mouth shut and let the boys make a hero out of me! At last I'm even with those Monarch sons, and I'm makin' it stick."

Cole washed his hands at the horse trough behind the Acme, thanked them and went back to town through the alleys. Already there was a commotion out on the street which announced the crowd had spotted Keen in the Acme archway.

He had been saved this time—saved by the generosity of ten strangers, all leagued with him in their hatred of Monarch. But that was luck. It wouldn't be that way again. Through his fog of weariness he was trying to remember what Keen had said about

Celia. Besides the other. "She come over to Craig this mornin' trying to beg us off you." Celia couldn't have done that.

Wearily he climbed the steps to the house. Halfway up the stairs Celia came out the door in her street clothes and hat. Seeing him, she stopped and then exclaimed, "Cole, what's happened to your face?"

Cole steadied himself on the railing. "Celia, did you see Craig Armin this mornin'?"

"Why—yes. Who told you?"

"Did you try to beg him off? Did you ask him to leave me alone?"

Celia's eyes flashed. "I did not, Cole Armin! I told him we were foolish to fight, that we ought to divide the field. When he refused I told him he was signing his own death warrant!" She looked magnificent, standing there, her face flushed and a little bit of concern behind the outrage in her eyes.

Cole said, "Thanks, Celia. That's all I want to know."

The sound of horses galloping pulled Cole's glance around toward the alley.

He saw Juck ride in the compound gate, and behind him was Girard, the China Boy super. They slipped from the saddle at the same time and tramped across the yard. Juck saw Cole first, and he stopped, and Girard looked up.

"Cole, it looks like we're done for," Girard said. "They knocked my watchman in the head last night, loaded a skip with black powder and caved in the last three galleries of the China Boy. There won't be any ore to haul out."

15

Sheriff Ed Linton had long ago sent Keen Billings on to his hotel in a spring wagon and was endlessly questioning Mort Cornwall, the Acme owner, when one of his deputies rode up and asked to speak with him. Linton drew off to one side of the wagon yard, conversed with his deputy a moment, then came back to Cornwall. Cornwall was surrounded by his grim teamsters; his shirt was torn; his hands were bloody, and the whip he had used was still lying in the dust before him.

"I've got to go, Cornwall, but I'll come back to you," Linton said.

"Come ahead," Cornwall said stubbornly. "If you aim to arrest me git it over with. But I'd like to see you make it stick."

"That's pretty rough treatment on a trespasser," Linton said sternly. "Too rough entirely."

"But it wasn't no ordinary trespasser," Cornwall countered promptly. "The Monarch run my business to the wall, Sheriff. They killed my father-in-law. And now they got the gall to come down here and try to bully me into sellin' them wagons so Western won't get 'em." He laughed shortly. "A horsewhip-ain't half rough enough if you ask me."

"You nearly killed a man."

"A damn pity I did such a sloppy job," Cornwall said.

Sheriff Linton turned on his heel, exasperation plain in his face, mounted his horse and joined his deputy.

Outside the yard, riding toward the center of town, Linton said to his harried-looking deputy, "Where's Girard now?"

"I dunno. Likely rousin' the town."

"You say there were four men killed in the explosion?"

"That's right."

"And he's sure it happened that way?"

"That's right. One of the miners workin' night shift got took sick. He was waitin' for the cage when this powder-loaded skip come by him at the gate. He gave a yell down a winze into the gallery below, and all them men down there run for the winze into the higher gallery. Four of 'em was workin' a stope, though, and they got buried. That gallery and the two below it where the day shift was workin' was plumb caved in."

Sheriff Linton's face was pale. They were in the town's afternoon traffic now, and he gave his horse its head and let it pick its way through the snarl of traffic on the main street.

"I don't see how it was done," he said finally to his deputy. "Somebody on top must have seen who did it."

"Hunh-unh. On night shift the gradin' shed is closed down. The ore skips is tripped into a big storage crib to be unloaded in the mornin'. The only man workin' on the top is the hoistman, and he's night watchman too. They slugged him, broke into the powder shed, and while the hull damn camp was sleepin' they loaded the skip, put a long fuse to the stuff and let her go down, then rode off."

At the sheriff's office Linton didn't even dismount. "Hunt Girard up and talk to him. When he's calmed down enough to talk send for me." He remembered something then and said, "Did you say 'they'?"

"What?" the deputy asked blankly.

"How many men did the job? You said they slugged him over the head."

"He don't know," the deputy replied. "I just figured it would take more than one of 'em—Monarch men, I reckon."

"Ah-h-h!" Linton snarled and pulled his horse around into the street. Here it was again. Four men dead in a mine explosion and again the finger of suspicion pointed toward Monarch. Toward Keen Billings in particular. Could Keen have ridden out there last night and done it? He could have. He would have had the time— but barely enough. But did he? Linton shook his head, silently voicing his denial. No, Billings wouldn't have done it, for he was afraid now. Then who did?

At Billings' hotel, the Piute, Linton dismounted and went into the lobby.

"Billings been brought in yet?" he asked the clerk.

"They carried him up a little while ago," the clerk said. "What happened?"

"He tripped on a match," Linton snarled.

He climbed the stairs, found Billings' room and knocked. There was a muffled sound in answer, and he went in. Billings was lying on the bed, the remains of his shirt off. His thick-muscled body was a mass of welts and bruises and cuts. His face, when he raised his head to look at Linton, was so swollen that it reminded Linton of soft, unset dough.

"Did you get him?" Billings groaned.

"You were trespassing," Linton said sternly. "He warned you off, and you stuck there. He was standing on his rights, Keen."

"Who?"

"Who what?"

"Who was standing on his rights?"

"Cornwall, you lughead."

It was a struggle for Keen Billings to sit up, but he did. Then he said in a voice filled with wrath, "You damn fool, Cornwall didn't beat me up! Cole Armin did!"

Linton stared at him and then smiled beneath his mustache. "You're loco, Keen. Cornwall beat you up."

"Armin did, I tell you!" Billings shouted. "Don't you think I know who I was fightin'?"

"No, I don't," Linton countered. "Cornwall had the shirt ripped off him. There was blood on his face and his hands. He'd been in a rough and tumble if I ever saw a man who was." He paused. "You sure you feel all right, Keen?"

Billings swore blisteringly. "It's a frame-up, Ed—a frame-up, I tell you." He told, between curses of his attempted deal with Cornwall, of Cole's entrance, of his words with Cole and of finally remembering the peace bond. But he had gone too far. How was he to know that Armin was sweet on Wallace's sister? That had brought on the fight, and he had been horsewhipped.

Linton listened carefully and then said, "But, dammit, Cornwall and his teamsters all claimed Cornwall fought you!"

"They're shieldin' Armin!" Billings yelled. "Go arrest him and get him out of the way!"

Linton shook his head slowly. "No chance, Keen—not with nine men calling me a liar I don't arrest Cole Armin. I want to stay sheriff here long enough to get our business done. He wouldn't stand for an arrest now anyway. He'd fight first—after what's happened."

"This scrap, you mean? He come off winner, so what's——"

"I don't mean this scrap," Linton said grimly. "I'm talkin' about somethin' else. I don't think you'll like to hear it either."

Billings looked carefully at him, warned by the expression on the sheriff's face.

"What?"

"Where were you last night from eleven o'clock on?" he asked.

"You ought to know," Billings said slowly, warily. "We sat in a game for an hour."

"And after that?"

"I come to bed." He was still watching Linton, sensing something was wrong. "Why?"

Linton said grimly, "Somebody slugged the hoistman at the China Boy last night. They loaded the skip with powder, lowered it, blew in three galleries of the China Boy and killed four men." He added dryly, "So the Western's China Boy contract ain't worth the paper it's written on for four-five months."

Billings was utterly motionless for a moment, and then he scrambled off the bed and lunged for the door. He locked it, then raced for the window shade and pulled it down. Then he said hoarsely, "Where's Cole Armin?"

"Scared, Keen?" Linton drawled, amusement in his voice.

"Is—is he comin' up here for me?" Billings asked huskily.

"Not that I know of."

"Listen," Billings said. "You go down in the lobby. When you see him come in you hold him off until I have time enough."

"For what?"

"To get out of here!" Billings said hoarsely. He dived into the closet. From out of it he threw a war bag and a pile of clothes and boots. When he came out again Linton was leaning against the foot of the bed. He held a gun in his hand, a small pocket gun, and it was pointed at Billings.

"Sit down, Keen," he drawled.

Billings sank into a chair, his face a pasty gray under its bruises.

"Just sit there and think a minute," Linton said. "Just think."

Billings tried to speak and failed. He tried again and the words came this time. "All right, Ed. What?"

"You ain't pullin' out of here, Keen. What about our deal?"

"To hell with the deal!" Billings groaned.

"So you say. I don't. I say it's goin' through."

"But Armin will kill me! Ed, I swear I didn't blow up the China Boy! But he won't believe me! He'll kill me!"

"I'll hide you," Linton said calmly. "He can't kill you if he can't find you, Keen."

"Yuh," Billings said dully, staring at the floor. "Yuh, that's right."

Linton walked over to Billings and slapped him sharply across the face. "Damn you, Keen. Wake up! You're not dead yet, and you won't be if you listen to me." Still Keen didn't look up, and Linton said impatiently, "Got any whisky in the room?"

"In the top drawer," Billings said thickly. Linton pocketed the gun, got the whisky from the dresser, uncorked the bottle and handed it to Keen. "Take a long swig of that."

Keen, docile as a child, obeyed. His hands were trembling as he tilted the bottle. He took one drink and then another, and Sheriff Linton, his eyes cold and alert, watched him cynically. The whisky helped. Keen rubbed his eyes, shook his head and then said in a quiet voice, "I'm all right, Ed."

"Got over your scare?"

"No. Neither would you if all this was pointin' to you instead of me." He looked up at Ed. "I tell you, Ed, he'll hunt me down and kill me. He was killin' mad over that sawed brake lever. But this— why, hell, this finishes it."

Sheriff Linton laughed softly. "Sure it does, you fool. It almost finishes Western too. Now what's there left to do in the rest of our little scheme?"

"I dunno," Billings said dumbly.

"Get a hold on yourself!" Linton said sharply. "Our plan was to whittle both the Monarch and the Western down. All right, Western is whittled down. Now all we got to do is whittle Monarch down one more notch. And then Craig Armin will be where Western is now—and he'll play his last card. He'll call you in, pay you enough money to satisfy you and then tell you to wipe out Armin and Wallace."

"Ed," Billings said dully, "who blew up the China Boy?"

"Aren't you listenin', you fool!" Linton flared up. "Didn't you hear me?"

"I heard you," Billings said. He took another swig of whisky from the bottle. "All right. Go ahead."

"There isn't any more!" Linton said harshly. He walked over to Billings and again he slapped him savagely across the face. He did it twice, and when Billings ducked his head into his arms Linton backed off.

"My God, man, are you in a trance?" he raged.

"I'm all right, Ed. Quit it. Quit it, I tell you. I've heard every word you've said. You're right. You're dead right." He looked at him. "But can you hide me so Armin can't find me?"

"I can," Linton said sharply. "Do you think he's got eyes that can look through walls?"

"Maybe he has," Billings said. "He's got everything else."

"You've got a big, wide, woolly stripe of yellow up your back, Keen," Linton sneered. "That's your trouble."

"I guess it is," Keen agreed calmly.

"You won't go yellow on *me*, my friend," Linton said ominously. "I'll tell you what I'm going to do with you. I'm going to rent the room just ahead of this one. And you're goin' to stay in it. Cole Armin is goin' to look for you. And I'm goin' to stick with him the whole damn night until I prod him into a fight and jail him. And then do you know what you're goin' to do, my friend, while he's hunting you?"

"What?" There was a spark of interest in Keen's face now.

"You're goin' to take a greener and blast a shot at Craig Armin —a shot so close he'll think he's dead!"

Keen didn't say anything.

Linton went on: "That alibis Armin. He'll be in jail. But it also gets Craig Armin wild. It's the last shove. You'll get your orders from him tomorrow to take care of Cole and Ted Wallace. I'll free Cole Armin then." He leaned back against the dresser. "With Cole Armin free and Craig Armin wild we got what we're after at last. From there on in it's a downhill drag."

"I see," Billings said quietly.

Linton watched him with shrewd eyes, waiting for him to pick holes in the argument. But Keen didn't, because there weren't any holes. It was tight. It was nice. But there was just one thing wrong in the picture, and stubbornly Keen could not forget it.

"Look, Ed. Don't get sore now, will you? I want to ask you something."

"Go ahead."

Billings spread his hand and ticked off counts on his fingers. "First, Ted Wallace is shoved downstairs and his leg broke. Second, that brake lever on Armin's wagon is sawed. Third, the China Boy is blowed up, and four——"

"And all those things have helped us, haven't they?" Linton interrupted. "They made Western mad enough to burn the Monarch down. It made Armin mad enough to threaten your life and get a peace bond slapped on him so he couldn't fight us. What are you kickin' about?"

"I want to know who done it all!" Billings wailed. "So would you if you had to stay locked in a hotel room while Armin hunted you!"

"But what does it matter?" Linton insisted. "You're alive."

"I got a feelin'," Billings said gloomily.

"What?"

"Somebody has took this right out of our hands," he said, raising his gaze to Linton. "Somebody knows what we're tryin' to do. And before we can finish it we're goin' to get it."

"That's damn foolishness!" Linton said.

"It couldn't be you, workin' with somebody else, could it, Ed?" Billings said steadily.

"Be careful," Linton warned coldly.

"Because all this falls on me," Billings went on stubbornly. "I'm the ranahan that Cole Armin is huntin'!"

"You're Monarch's manager. Who else would he hunt? Not me."

"I just wondered," Billings said slowly. "It seems mighty damn queer."

"But not so queer you'll back out, Keen," Linton said, iron in his voice. "Because I've got enough to hang you, my friend, and you gave it to me—free. Remember who killed Joyce at Acme? Think that over."

They glared suspiciously at each other for a long moment, and then Billings' glance slid away. Linton said, "Wait right here till I rent this next room. Leave your clothes here, and move in next door. I'll be back in a minute."

He unlocked the door and stepped outside. In the hall, now darkening in the late-afternoon dusk, he paused and stared down the corridor. So Keen thought he was crossing him, selling him out. Linton hadn't thought of it before, but why not? Once Cole Armin and Wallace were dead what was to stop him from doing just that—getting Monarch for himself?

It was an idea anyway. He'd have to think it over. As he walked down the stairs he was smiling faintly under his silky and handsome mustache.

16

When Girard finished telling Ted Wallace of the China Boy explosion none of them—Cole, Celia, Juck or Ted—said anything immediately. There wasn't much to say anyway in the face of blank ruin.

"It's murder," Girard said. "I've got to face the families of those four men! And what can I tell them? That Monarch killed them, that the sheriff—even if he could get proof—is scared to use it and that all we can do is take it."

Ted said miserably, "You haven't got any ore on top that we could haul, Girard?"

"You know I haven't," Girard replied. "The mine was closed down until the Monarch's freightin' trial and yours."

Ted looked over at Celia. "Well, I reckon that does it. We're sunk. I don't know what the bank will do about my note. I borrowed on the face of your contract, Girard. They won't take it now. And I'll have to sell some of the wagons and stock for collateral for the money I borrowed for Cole's bond."

Cole, who was closest the door, went out into the living room. His war bag lay in the corner behind a chair, and he was squatting over it when Girard went out the door, announcing, "Well, I'm going to raise hell with that fancy-pants sheriff, Cole. Won't do any good though."

"I reckon not," Cole said quietly and Girard went down the steps.

Cole fumbled among his stuff and found his gun and belt. He had put them in there last night, hoping he wouldn't have to use them and afraid that he would. But last night the China Boy contract stood between Western and utter failure. Tonight it didn't. Nothing did. They were done.

He straightened up and started to put the gun belt on when he was aware of someone watching him. He wheeled, to see Celia standing by the door just inside the room.

"What's it going to get you, Cole?" Celia asked quietly.

"I'd sort of like to leave my mark anyway," Cole drawled. "When Ted gets enough money saved again to start Western he's not goin' to have to fight Keen Billings."

"They'll get you," Celia said in a tight voice. "You can't fight a whole town, Cole!"

"Maybe." Cole picked up his hat.

Celia wanted to cry out, to stop him. She couldn't let him go this way, walking out to kill a man and be killed himself. But she wasn't going to stop him, she knew. There are times when a man's own code is in question, and he has to act according to his lights, foolish or suicidal or rash. And those times, if he is a man like Cole

Armin, there is no way a woman can stop him. He has to do it. Celia understood that when she said good-by to Cole, misery in her face.

Juck spoke from behind her. "I'll watch him, Miss Celia. He won't get in no trouble."

Celia shook her head. "It's no use, Juck. I know."

"What if he can't find Keen Billings?" Juck rumbled.

"But he will."

"Not if I get the word out to Keen in time," Juck said. He brushed past her, and he did not even see the faint glint of hope in her eyes.

For something happened to Celia then. If Juck could help that way she could help in another way.

Cole headed out into the street and down it, bound for the Piute Hotel and Keen Billings. It was almost a relief now to have this worry over, to know that the worst had happened. Not quite the worst, however. The worst would be having Keen Billings go free. Cole felt calm, his nerves keyed up and screwed tight, and they would be that way until it was over. For it never occurred to Cole that it wasn't Keen Billings who blew in the China Boy.

The town was just lighting up, but the Piute Hotel lobby was dark when he entered it.

At his entrance a man rose from one of the lobby chairs and said, "Lookin' for someone, Armin?"

Cole hauled up, and Sheriff Linton strolled over to him, a half-smile on his face. Something warned Cole to go a little easy now if he was to play out his string. He said amiably, "Yeah, I'm glad you stopped me, Linton. I have a couple of questions to ask."

"Go ahead," Linton drawled.

"How do I go about breakin' my peace bond?" Cole asked gently. "I mean, what have I got to do to forfeit it?"

"Just get in another ruckus like you were in this afternoon," Linton said easily. "Only I doubt if you can find a half-dozen men to lie for you like you did today."

Cole smiled without humor. "That worked nice, didn't it?"

Linton nodded. "Pretty nice. But it won't work again."

"You didn't answer my question," Cole reminded him.

"I'll answer it this way," Sheriff Linton said slowly. "You can hunt Keen Billings, and if you find him you can choose him. But when you go for your gun—and it don't matter if he goes first, because you'll rawhide him into it—you're fair game. You're dead, in fact."

Cole looked searchingly in his eyes. "Maybe," he said softly.

"No maybe about it. I'm stickin' close to you tonight, Armin. You won't have a prayer of gettin' away with it."

"I'll take a chance," Cole said. "Where is he?"

"Suppose you find him," Linton suggested.

"Suppose I do," Cole answered, a reckless light in his eyes. He went over to the desk, inquired for Billings' room number and was given it. Linton followed him up the stairs and paused beside him as he knocked on Billings' door. There was no answer. Cole opened the door and looked into the room. It was dark in here. He walked across to the window, pulled the shade and looked around him.

Linton, lounging in the door, said, "This is against the law, of course, but we'll overlook that."

"Thanks," Cole said without looking at him. He opened the closet door. Billings was gone but not for good. His clothes lay in a heap in the middle of the floor.

"Well, there's other places," Cole murmured. "A rum head like Billings won't stay out of a saloon long."

Linton shrugged. He followed Cole downstairs and out on the street and paused at his elbow when Cole stopped to consider where next to look. Piute was too big to search house by house, but it wasn't too big to search bar by bar. Besides, the word would get around. All he would have to do would be to start it, and someone would flush Billings.

The first bar was a small one, but he inquired of the bartender for Keen Billings. When told he wasn't there Cole said, "Tell him Cole Armin is lookin' for him, will you, if you see him?"

The bartender smiled knowingly, looked at the sheriff with a puzzled expression and said, "Sure."

By the time Cole, with Linton trailing him, was three saloons further up the street the word was ahead of him. When he approached the barkeep in this bar and opened his mouth to speak the bartender said, "Sure. I'll tell him," and then laughed along with the crowd at the bar.

Sheriff Linton was annoyed, but he tried to pass it off as a joke. The next bar Cole went in was the Desert Dust. The freighters were just off the day shift, and they were drinking up. At Cole's entrance he received an ovation. More than one teamster from the

Monarch joined in too. Juck was standing back among them, and he grinned at sight of Cole. The teamsters gathered around Cole and Sheriff Linton, and Cole asked, "Anybody seen Billings?"

There was general laughter at that. Then one teamster said, "Who's the dude with you, Cole?"

Sheriff Linton wheeled and said, "Who said that?"

"I did," a teamster behind him said.

Before Linton could get turned around another voice said, "You're a liar. I did."

Linton's face was angry. He said, "I won't take any lip from you men! Understand that, for once an' all!"

They were big men, and Sheriff Linton was of medium size and dapper. Minus the badge, which he scorned to wear, his brag was ridiculous, and these men knew it. It gave one irreverent teamster an idea.

"Who are you, runt?" he asked.

Sheriff Linton glared at him. "I'll give you the benefit of the doubt, my man, just in case you really don't know. I'm the sheriff."

"Where's your star?" another man asked.

"He's braggin'," a third said.

"Make him prove it," a fourth said.

Linton looked from one to the other, unable to pin any of them down. And then, just as he was getting ready to speak, somebody reached over his shoulder, grabbed his hat and pulled it down over his eyes.

Two other huskies picked him up by the collar of his coat and the seat of his pants, took a run and threw him through the bat-wing doors. There was a second of silence, then a crash as a tie rail split and a solid thud on the ground.

When Sheriff Linton, his face livid with rage, burst through the doors a moment later, his pocket gun in his fist, every man in the room was innocently lined up at the bar, eying the door.

"Stand back there!" he snarled. "Line up and give me your guns!"

One teamster turned ostentatiously to his neighbor and said, "I heard a hell of a good joke today."

"What was it?" his neighbor asked.

And as one man the teamsters took their drinks, turned their backs to Sheriff Linton and listened to the joke. Linton yelled at them and bawled at them. He even let loose with a shot into the floor that nobody paid any attention to. And finally, not daring to arrest the whole saloon and not wishing to risk further assault to his dignity, he backed out the door and vanished.

One teamster spat and said, "He ain't even half a man without he's got a couple of deputies on each arm."

Cole looked over at Juck, and Juck avoided his glance. This was Juck's work, he knew, and he only shook his head.

A teamster asked seriously, "Anything we can do, Cole?"

"Nothin'," Cole said. "Thanks, boys."

He went out the door, and immediately Sheriff Linton fell in beside him. Cole stopped and murmured, "Ain't you had enough, Linton?"

"Armin, tomorrow I'm goin' to close up that saloon and fine the owner! Now get along!"

"I believe you'd do it," Cole said contemptuously.

"I will. Are you still goin' through with this?"

Cole wheeled and started up street, not bothering to answer. He was beginning to worry now about Billings showing up. If it were left to Billings, he knew, he would run. But Billings and Monarch aimed to live in this town and be part of it. And to save his face, his reputation for toughness, and to prove that he was a better man than any Western could put forward, Billings would have to show, sooner or later. He might choose to do it from ambush or turn it into a surprise, but it would have to be done if he were to stay in Piute. Cole was counting on that.

Four more saloons, and Cole knew that the word had been out long since. A crowd tagged at his heels now, the morbidly curious, the people who loved to see gun fights and bloodshed. Cole hated it, but in a way it would help. Sooner or later Billings would walk out of a saloon, and the crowd would scatter and they would shoot it out.

It was at Womack's Keno Parlor, a big saloon that was the hangout of the better-paid working men like Keen Billings, that Cole saw two deputies from Linton's office at the bar, facing the room, their elbows resting on the bar edge. They were two huskies, long-jawed and big, with the brutal faces and cynical eyes of men who are peace officers but little concerned with justice. They looked at Sheriff Linton, their boss, ready to take their cue from him. And Sheriff Linton looked mussed and dusty and wholly angry. That was enough.

"You still on the prod?" the first deputy sneered, eying Cole. "You want to watch out, mister. Somebody'll pull a gun on you and you'll faint."

"It won't be you, pardner," Cole said mildly and spoke to the bartender. "Billings been in?"

"Ain't seen him," the bartender said sourly.

"Tell him I'm lookin' for him," Cole said, mouthing the familiar and hopeful formula.

The first deputy, meanwhile, had looked over at Linton, and Linton, his anger still at the boiling point, nodded. He'd have to make his chance now, for they were coming to the last of the saloons. He signed the deputy to go ahead.

The deputy, when Cole was finished, said, "Maybe I better take that gun away from you, Armin. You'll hurt yourself."

"And maybe you better not," Cole said, glancing over at the sheriff. He knew he was going to break his bond, but he wanted it to count—with Billings.

Sheriff Linton shrugged. "I don't care much one way or the other."

The deputy snapped his fingers. "Hand it over."

"Wait a minute," Cole said slowly. "Have I said what I wanted of Billings?"

"You don't need to."

"But I haven't. So you boys whistle. I haven't broke any peace bond, fella. And any man has got a right to carry a gun in this town." He tilted his head toward Linton. "Ask him."

"He said he didn't care, brother," the deputy said, color flushing up into his full neck. "I do. Hand it over."

"But I care, too," Cole drawled. "And as long as the sheriff don't, why I reckon I'll keep it."

The deputy reached out and cuffed Cole across the mouth with the back of his hand, and there was a smile on his cynical face. He had it wiped off immediately, for Cole cuffed him back and hard enough to break the skin of his lip.

The deputy stood for a full second, blank astonishment on his face. And then he swung heavily at Cole's face. Cole ducked, caught him off balance and put both hands in his midriff and shoved him back into the arms of his fellow deputy.

"Go careful, Big Wind," Cole said mildly. "If I bust this peace bond I aim to make it count with a gun."

The deputy, now on his feet, looked at Linton, whose hand was in his pocket. Linton wasn't looking at him but was watching Cole for the first move.

And the deputy, who was in the habit of shooting first and talking later, grabbed for his gun. Cole's hand streaked for his. Sheriff Linton whipped his gun out of his pocket and rapped Cole across the skull. And the second deputy knocked the first deputy's arm up, so that his shot crashed into the bar mirror.

Cole melted to the floor, his gun clattering from his unconscious hand.

"Well, he broke his bond all right," Linton said grimly, standing over him. "I knew he would."

And because this was the hangout of the deputies and Keen Billings nobody demurred.

The first deputy, spitting blood from a cut lip, picked Cole up by his feet, the other by his head. Linton cleared the way as they carried him out of the saloon, dragging him in the dust as they ducked under the hitch racks on either side of the street, and into the sheriff's office.

Linton opened the door at the rear of the office that let into the cell block. A drunk was sleeping off a jag in the first cell. Linton unlocked the cell door with the big key ring, and his deputies threw Cole on the cot. They were standing there, looking at him, as the blast of a shotgun lifted over the racket of the town.

Linton turned his head. "That was a greener!"

His two deputies ran for the door and left him alone with Cole. Linton stood there a long time, looking down at Cole. Then, his face twisted with hatred, Linton slashed him across the face with the keys, leaving a cut in his cheek.

Afterward, feeling better, he closed the door and went out.

Letty was standing by the compound gate in the alley, wondering whether to risk it or not, when she saw Celia open the door and slip out. Celia came down the steps, walked out of the compound and went down the alley, her stride purposeful.

Letty waited until she was out of sight, then she walked slowly into the compound, as if undecided about something. When she passed into the glow of the lantern hanging on the gate an observer could have seen indecision in her face—and doubt. This was her chance. Cole Armin was on the prowl, and Celia had gone out. It would never be easier. She remembered Ted's face, how fiercely he defended her to Celia, and the memory made a warm glow inside her. She was a fool for treasuring this, she knew, and she was only hurting herself. But Ted had been kind to her and so had Celia. Yet there was the memory of Pete, and thinking of him was like twisting the knife in her wound.

She gazed up at the lighted window, and then suddenly she seemed to make up her mind. She looked behind her, saw the alley and compound were deserted, and then she climbed the steps, knocked gently on the door and walked in.

Ted had heard the door open, and he put his gun back under the covers when Letty stepped into the room. A smile broke on his gloomy face.

"Letty!"

"I had to come," Letty said quickly. "I wondered if there was anything I could do."

"Sit down," Ted said. He watched her hungrily as she took the chair beside his bed.

"The word is all over town about our losing the contract. Will—does it make any difference to Western, Ted?"

Ted laughed bitterly. "All the difference in the world. With it we could have pulled through. Without it—well, I don't know."

"Are we finished then? Is Western done for?" Letty tried to ask it casually, but she couldn't. She was hoping against hope that he would say yes so that she could take back the word to Keen Billings and Craig Armin and be done with this.

Ted looked at her and said, "Who said so?"

"I just wondered."

"I'm not licked," Ted said quietly. "I'm just back where I started. I've got a new wagon yard and more wagons. Not enough wagons, but they'll have to do. And we start all over again."

Ted fell quiet, staring at the dark window, and Letty watched him for a moment. "What are you thinking?" she asked.

Ted smiled wryly. "I was thinking about when I came in here with one wagon, six mules and a lot of ambition."

A shadow of pain crossed Letty's face. She was thinking of another man who had come into Piute the same way—her brother Pete. She said dully, "I knew a man who did that too. Only he didn't have your luck."

Ted looked at her. "Who was that?"

"My brother Pete."

"What happened to him?" Ted said.

Letty looked at him, looked him straight in the eye. "He died," she said. "Someone slipped a kingbolt on his wagon, and his wagon went wild. He broke both legs and died of gangrene."

Ted put out his hand and touched hers. "I'm sorry, Letty. I didn't know."

Letty's body was taut as he touched her. Was he acting? He was, of course, for he had slipped Pete's kingbolt. He had killed Pete. She had to keep telling herself this because it straightened her back and somehow made this a little less awful. But deep within her she knew that it was destroying part of her. She was weak and disgusting, not even a good hater. Even the memory of Pete and how he died couldn't keep her from going soft when she saw Ted Wallace. Grimly, then, she remembered what she had come for.

"It doesn't matter," she said dully. "Only it taught me a lesson, Ted."

"What?"

"This freighting business is the most hateful business in the world! It breaks men and kills them and forgets them and doesn't care, just so the ore gets out! Just so a company can abide by a contract!"

"Why, Letty," Ted said, surprised at her vehemence, "I didn't know you felt that way about it."

"I do," Letty said. "That—well, that's half why I came up here tonight."

"To tell me that?"

"To ask why you and Mr. Armin don't quit, don't get out of it, while you still have a little money left."

There it was, and Letty watched him. She had made her plea on two grounds, and her sincerity as Ted watched her couldn't be doubted. She hoped Western would quit so that she could break with Billings before something terrible happened. Her other reason was more obscure, and she would scarcely admit it to herself. But dark intuition warned her that something would happen to Ted if he didn't and that she would be the cause of it too.

Ted's face was puzzled as he studied hers. Then he said, "I don't work that way, Letty. Cole doesn't either."

"What have you to look forward to?" Letty asked quickly.

"Why—we started from the bottom once. I did. I can do it

again. We've got a lot to look forward to. Beating Monarch, for one thing."

"But you can't, Ted! Don't you see that?"

"Why can't we?"

Letty made a hopeless gesture. "They have money! They have gunmen! They have the sheriff! How can you fight those three?"

"I dunno," Ted said slowly. "But we will."

"And be alive in the end to tell the tale? No, you won't, Ted. I know it!"

Ted smiled and said gently, "Are you scared, Letty?"

"Not for myself. For you."

Ted put a hand on hers. Letty knew, by the look in his face and his eyes, that he was going to say something that she couldn't let him say. She drew her hands away quickly and said, "I'm thinking of Celia, Ted. What would she do?"

"If what?"

"If you get—if the same thing happens to you that happened to my brother." Letty's eyes were dark and afraid and bitter. "Ted, I don't know how else to say it. You'll laugh at me and call me a woman. But I know I'm right." She paused. "Something terrible is going to happen to us, Ted—all of us in Western."

"Why do you say that?"

"I can't explain it. Call it intuition if you will."

"It sounds like a warning," Ted said laughing.

"Then call it that!" Letty said vehemently. "Then take my warning!"

Ted stared at her, puzzled. "Letty, do you know something?"

Letty's face drained of color. She stood up and said, "No! No! How could I? All I know is that I have an uneasy feeling about us, Ted. It's something I can't fight. And if I could I would make you send for Craig Armin tonight and have a talk with him. He'd buy you out and be glad to. And then you'd be rid of this—this monster of a freighting business!"

Ted looked down at his hands and then slowly shook his head.

"No. It's gone too far now, Letty. Someday—I don't know how or when—Craig Armin is comin' to me with a proposition to sell Monarch. I'll stick until he does."

Letty sighed. "I knew you'd say that. I was sure of it."

"What else could I say?"

Letty didn't know. She stood there, looking down at Ted, and he was looking at her when the sound of gunshot, heavy and distinct over the racket of the town, came to them.

"Who would be shootin' a shotgun at this hour of night?" Ted wondered audibly.

Keen Billings, after Cole and Sheriff Linton had finished prowling in his room and gone, sat down weakly on the bed and waited for his heart to stop hammering. He didn't even like to be that close to Cole Armin. He was sore and hurt all over from the beating he had received this afternoon, and the whisky wasn't helping him much now. But he kept on drinking until it was dark, lying on the bed, a water glass of whisky in his big hand, his legs spread wide on the bed. His mind was a confused tangle of thoughts and memories, but the one that recurred most often and nagged at him was the one he hated most. Who blew up the China Boy? He wished desperately that he could answer that and regain a certain peace of mind.

Patiently then, because he had the time, he thought about this. And shrewdly he chose the sawing of the brake lever as the key to it.

Four people knew about Jim Rough being hired—himself, Linton, Letty Burns and Craig Armin. When he said Craig Armin's name to himself he cursed him. His pay check would come tomorrow—half pay this time, less than his best teamster earned. The memory of Craig Armin's face was enough to make Billings mad. But it wouldn't be long now. Just a short wait, and then Craig Armin would have the dirty end of the stick. And how he would squirm!

Billings put this from his mind and returned to considering the four people who knew about Jim Rough. He knew that he didn't saw the brake lever, so he was out. Linton, working through someone else, might have done it. But why would Linton risk getting Cole Armin mad enough to kill him, Billings, when Linton needed him for this future job? No, Linton was out too. Now Letty. She could have done it through somebody else too. But why would she do it, and how did she stand to profit by it? She didn't, so he could count her out.

That left Craig Armin, damn him! He wouldn't do it, because he always left those dirty, stinking jobs for Billings to do. He was too fine mannered, too delicate, too damn superior for a job like that!

So he was out too. And Billings was right back where he started then. He didn't know.

He heaved himself to his feet, now that it was really dark, and he found that he was pretty drunk—too drunk. Pouring out a basin of water, he washed his face in it and then soaked his head. When he had dried himself he found it had helped. But he was still too drunk. He'd have to take extra care tonight.

He put on a shirt, vest, hat and his gun belt and slipped out of the room. From the top of the stairs he could see that few people were in the lobby. He hurried down the stairs, turned and walked down the corridor past the dining room and out the rear entrance that led onto an alley.

Out there in the night somewhere Cole Armin was hunting him, and that meant he couldn't show himself. He had a pretty accurate knowledge of Piute and, using that and his instinct, he kept to the alleys and within half an hour was at the rear of the sheriff's office. He had met none who knew him.

There was a rain barrel under the downspout back of the jail, and Billings walked up to it and stuck his hand inside. There was the sawed-off shotgun, just where Linton had said it would be. He pulled it out, broke it and pocketed the shell. Then he took the gun apart, stuck the barrel inside one trouser leg, the stock inside the other, tightened his belt to hold them, pulled the points of his vest over his belt and walked down the alley.

He paused at the rear entrance of the Cosmopolitan House, fixing it in his mind. Opening the door cautiously, he peered inside. There was a big storage room immediately inside the door, and beyond that a closed door that led into a corridor that ran straight through into the lobby. He wasn't concerned with that corridor, however, for there were service stairs opening off this storeroom that led to the floor above. A lamp in a wall bracket was turned down low in the storeroom, and Billings slipped inside the door. He walked softly to the service stairs, opened the door, saw nothing but a dark well and closed the door after him.

He was a third of the way up the stairs when the door at the top opened and a maid, sheets under her arm, stepped down the stairs, closing the door behind her. Billings froze against the wall, held his breath, sucked in his chest and waited. The maid passed him, the cloth of her dress sleeve touching him, and went downstairs. She opened the door, then looked back up the stairs, curiosity on her face. She had smelled a distinct odor of whisky. But the lamp in the storeroom threw no light up the stairs, and Keen remained immobile.

When she shut the door he let out his breath.

"I'm lucky tonight," he thought.

He went up the stairs and stepped out into the carpeted corridor. He was safe here he knew. He walked toward the front of the building and climbed the stairs to the next story. Craig Armin's suite was in the rear corner, a big living room on the end, then the study and then the bedroom behind them along the side of the building. Craig Armin would probably be in the living room.

Keen walked to the end of the corridor and looked out the open window. Just below him was a lighted window, the window of Craig Armin's study. Below it was a wide ledge of limestone which formed the sill of all the windows on the first story. But Billings wasn't counting on that. There was a heavy coil of knotted rope by this window, the fire escape for the third floor. That was all he'd need.

He took the rope and threw it out into the night. It snaked down, uncoiling, and touched the ground. He heard footsteps coming down the corridor. Calmly he leaned out the window, as if watching the night, until the sound of footsteps turned into a room and the door closed.

Then he brought the shotgun out, put it together, loaded it, swung a leg over the sill, then both legs, and silently lowered himself to the ledge below. Coming to a rest, he squatted down, holding the rope. He peered through the curtains, hoping that the room was empty.

But what he saw brought a smile to his face. Craig Armin sat at his study desk, and in a chair before him was Celia Wallace. The window was closed, so that he could not hear what they were saying. But through the gauzy curtains he could see them very plainly. Craig Armin was embarrassed; he was pulling his ear as he listened to Celia Wallace. Suddenly Celia Wallace stood up, talking. Craig Armin came to his feet, said something very slowly, then rapped the desk with his hand.

Celia Wallace turned, walked a few steps toward the door, then paused and spoke again.

Billings, holding onto the rope with a hand to brace himself, raised the shotgun to his shoulder and sighted it. He drew a bead on Craig Armin, and the impulse to pull the trigger then was almost overpowering. But he lifted the sights and waited. Craig Armin bowed and sat down. Billings, to make sure he followed Linton's orders only to scare him, raised the sights a little higher and pulled the trigger.

There was a smashing roar, and the gun kicked back, knocking him off balance. But the rope was there, and he held onto it, looking inside. There was a ragged hole in the curtains. On the paneling behind and the ceiling above Craig Armin was a wide circle of scarred wood. But Craig Armin was what he was looking at.

There was a tiny smear of blood welling on Craig Armin's cheek. Slowly, his terrified gaze on the window, Craig Armin raised a hand to his cheek. And then he dived under his desk.

Billings was satisfied. He dropped his gun, lowered himself down the rope, walked into the alley and down it, whistling slightly off key as he disappeared in the darkness.

When the crash of that shot pounded through the room Celia had her hand on the doorknob. She cried out involuntarily with fright, then wheeled in time to see Craig Armin, his face like a death mask, put a hand to his face, then dive under the desk.

The door was opened in her face then by the Chinese servant. He took one look at the empty desk and Craig Armin's hand showing beneath it, and then he ran into the foyer, threw open the door and screamed.

After that men—all kinds of men—poured into Craig Armin's study, racing past her.

Slowly Craig Armin came up from behind the desk and pointed to the window.

"Some—somebody tried to kill me," he announced in a faint voice. A man poked his head through the paneless window, saw the rope and yelled, "He's got away! Down the fire escape!"

There was pandemonium then. Celia never realized how helpless men like these, not used to blood or emergencies, were. Craig Armin's face was bleeding a little but no more than from a razor cut during his morning shave. Yet men were bawling for a doctor, shouting at each other, giving contradictory orders and making a general mess of things when two deputies from Sheriff Linton's office entered.

The men parted at their entrance, and Craig Armin announced dramatically, "I was shot at!"

And then his glance fell on Celia by the door. He raised his hand and pointed. "Arrest that woman!"

There was utter silence for a moment, and then one of the deputies, looking from Celia to Craig Armin, said, "She shoot you, Mr. Armin?"

"No. But I know who did. And she was sent here as a decoy!"

The deputy looked politely doubtful. He said, "You say you know who shot you?"

"I do. Cole Armin."

The deputy shook his head. "I'm afraid you're wrong, Mr. Armin. Cole Armin is in jail."

Craig Armin's face sagged, but Celia didn't see that. She said to the deputy in a choked, faint voice, "Then—he got Billings?"

"No ma'am," the deputy said. "He made the mistake of thinkin' he could lick two deputies and the sheriff."

"Thank God," Celia whispered. "Thank God."

17

Sheriff Linton was an early caller at Craig Armin's suite next morning. He was in an immaculate black suit; his linen was white and starched; he was freshly barbered and, all in all, looked elegant. He was shown into the big living room of Craig Armin's suite, where Armin was just finishing breakfast.

"Good morning, Armin. You sent for me?"

"Sit down," Craig Armin said curtly. He didn't bother to offer Linton a cup of coffee but waved his breakfast away. As soon as the servant was gone Armin took out a cigar, lighted it, and rose. There was a fresh neat bandage on his cheek, where one of the buckshot had nicked him.

"Linton," he began, "I understand you've got my nephew in jail."

"That's right," Linton said easily.

"On what grounds?"

"For breaking peace bond. He tried to beat up on me and my deputies."

Armin, standing at the window that overlooked the street, now turned to regard Linton. "Will you keep him there?"

Linton shook his head. "I'm afraid I can't, Mr. Armin."

"Why not?"

"What's his crime? He'll be haled before the judge this morning, fined twenty-five dollars and freed—and, of course, forfeit his peace bond."

Craig Armin puffed nervously at his cigar. "You're sure you arrested him last night before that shot was fired at me?"

"Positive." A faint trace of a smile was playing around the corners of Linton's mouth, but Craig Armin's back was turned. "I was standing over him in the cell when I heard the shot and sent my deputies."

Armin grunted. Then he said quietly, "I want him kept in jail, Linton. His men shot at me, you know."

Linton smiled then, a secret, wise smile. "But *he* didn't," Linton pointed out. "I can't do it, Mr. Armin. I'd like to oblige, but I can't."

"For, say, a thousand dollars?" Craig Armin murmured and turned to look at him.

Linton shook his head. "If I held him past noon some jackleg lawyer would be in court with a writ. I'd be on the pan for fair."

"I see," Armin said. He looked out the window, musing. "There isn't any other charge against him you could bring up?"

Linton pretended to think, although he was quite certain what he would say.

"None," he said presently. "No matter what I suspect him of I have to get proof. Personally I think he set the fire at your place, but there was that girl to alibi him. I couldn't arrest him, so I did the next best thing: I put him on peace bond. No, I can't hold him for anything else."

"He destroyed a buckboard of mine," Armin insisted. "Can't he be held for that?"

Linton smiled pleasantly. "Between us, Mr. Armin, Billings asked for that beating. He didn't obey the flag signal."

"Yes, yes," Armin said hurriedly.

Linton settled back in his chair. He was enjoying this. Slowly, thread by thread, he was weaving his web around Craig Armin. He could almost see Armin's decision slowly crystallize. He could follow Armin's every thought. Right now Craig Armin was sounding him out to see if there wasn't some possibility of keeping Cole Armin in jail, figuring this move, for once and all, would break Cole Armin and Western. Failing that, Linton was sure enough of what would follow. Craig Armin was scared to death, and when a man like that is scared he does reckless things.

Craig said gloomily, "Well, if you can't you can't."

"I'd like to oblige," Linton said smoothly, "but it can't be done." He paused, wanting what he was going to say next to sink in. "I know your position, Armin. You're fighting a bunch of lawless bully boys. Personally I think if you give them enough rope they'll hang themselves. I've got my eye on them. At the first chance I get I'm going to jail them." He shrugged. "Of course you're not in a pleasant position," he said slyly. "They may get you before I get them."

Craig Armin's face drained of color. "Exactly," he said.

"But that's a chance we have to take on the frontier. A lawman is helpless. Every man is innocent until proven guilty. It's only *after* the crime is done that I can act. Before, even though I can see it coming, I can do nothing. The law doesn't back me up." He rose, watching Armin's tortured face. He couldn't resist the last turn of the screw. "I'd certainly be careful from now on, Armin. Keep a man with you all the time."

Armin shakily wiped the sweat from his forehead with a fine linen handkerchief.

"I will," he said. "That reminds me. Have you seen Keen Billings this morning?"

"I'll run into him, I suspect," Linton said. "I'll send him up."

"Thanks," Armin murmured. He got a hold on himself and managed a smile. "Well—I can raise that ante to five thousand," he said abruptly.

Linton shook his head and smiled. "I'd like to, Mr. Armin, but it can't be done. No sir, it can't be done."

They shook hands, and Linton noticed that Craig Armin's palm was wet. That shot last night had put the fear of God into him. Linton chuckled with anticipation as he went downstairs and out onto the street.

He could free Cole Armin now. No, on the other hand, he'd better give Keen time enough to get to Craig Armin before he did that. Cole Armin would still be on the prod, more so than ever, he supposed.

At the Piute he waved a cheery good morning to the clerk and went upstairs. Keen Billings, still in his new room, opened the door.

"Well?" he asked.

Linton closed the door behind him and then laughed out loud. Billings grinned and said, "Come on. What did he say?"

"He's so scared he can't talk," Linton said. "I warned him to be careful and hire a bodyguard, and he almost fainted."

"The hell he did," Billings said and laughed.

"He offered me five thousand dollars to keep Cole Armin in jail, just like I knew he would."

"Then he is scared," Billings said dryly. "If he puts out that much money he's scared."

"He wants you," Linton said.

"Already, huh? Then you must have did a good job, Ed."

"You'll see," Linton said. "Now get along. I'll give you time to get to the hotel before I turn Cole Armin loose."

Billings' smile suddenly faded. "Yeah. Cole Armin." He hitched up his pants and said, "Well, I only got to worry about that ranahan a few hours more."

"That's right," Linton said. "When you see Armin you know how to play it. We've talked that over. Afterward, after dark, you can tell me how it's goin' to come off."

"Yeah," Billings said. His mouth curled in a cruel smile. "Now I can watch that coyote squirm. But tonight, after it's over, is what I been waitin' to see. I been thinkin' about it all the time, dreamin' about it, waitin' for it." He looked at Linton. "You let me handle him tonight after it's over, Ed. I've earned that, by God."

"Sure, sure," Linton said. "Now get along."

Billings picked up his Stetson and put it on. Linton said, as he was walking toward the door, "Don't forget to get his check, Keen. That's important. That's evidence that will help cinch the deal."

"I know, I know, sure," Billings said. "Gimme fifteen minutes."

Billings went down the stairs and headed for the Cosmopolitan House, whistling tunefully. It was a perfect Piute day, with the air still, the sun already hot, the smell of dust and manure and hot boards in the air. Passing the saloons, there was the cool, sweet smell of beer and freshly wet sawdust. Life was pretty good. And what made it good was that Craig Armin, damn his soul, was about to be put on a skewer and barbecued.

Craig Armin's attitude, when Keen was shown into the living room of his suite, was haughty and cold. That was a good sign, Keen reflected, as he sat down; it meant he wasn't sure of himself.

"You've been making yourself pretty scarce lately," Armin observed, letting himself down into the most comfortable chair.

"Damn right I have," Keen said bluntly. "I don't hone for a bellyful of lead from Cole Armin."

Craig Armin smiled faintly. "And I don't either, Keen. You heard about last night?"

Keen nodded. "That was pretty close, chief."

"I didn't like it," Armin said wryly. "The more I think of it the less I like it."

"They're startin' to play rough all right," Billings conceded grimly. "What the hell use is a freightin' business if you're scared to show your face to run it?"

"Keen, I'm going to put an end to this," Craig Armin said quietly.

"You are?" Keen said blankly. "How?"

"I should say 'we' are," Armin said. "You and I—both of us. We're both afraid of that outfit, if we tell the truth, aren't we?"

"I sure as hell am," Keen said with utter sincerity.

"Then let's wipe them out."

He and Armin looked at each other for a long moment. Then Keen said, "You mean, let's 'me' wipe them out, don't you, boss?"

"I'll pay you."

"Sure. Only no thanks."

"Losin' your guts, Keen?"

"I've already lost em," Keen grunted placidly.

"You're gettin' pretty coy all of a sudden, Keen," Armin said.

"You would be too."

"But I think you'll take this job," Armin said slowly.

"And I don't reckon I will."

They stared at each other levelly, and there was hatred in both their eyes. Finally Craig Armin smiled. "You didn't take that seriously the other night—what I said about cutting your pay?"

"How else could I take it?"

"I was angry," Armin said with a gesture of dismissal. "Forget it, Keen. You and I have gone through enough together that we can quarrel without hard feelings, haven't we?"

"Have we?" Keen said sulkily.

"Look here. I'll pay you. It's something you'll have to do anyway, sooner or later, if you want to live. Why not take pay for it?"

Billings pretended to consider this, his heavy face set in a scowl. If Craig Armin had been a little more observant he would have seen that Keen Billings' eyes were not quite so puzzled as he wanted them to appear.

"That's a fact," Billings said.

"A thousand dollars then?"

"No," Keen said quickly. "I'm riskin' my neck, chief—and I mean *riskin'*."

"Two thousand."

"Not for twice that."

"All right," Craig Armin said grimly. "I'll make it five—and I'll also give you the closest thing to an airtight alibi you can find."

Keen knew he didn't need any alibi, but the five thousand was satisfactory, so he pretended interest. Why fight over a little money when he would get half Craig Armin's in the end? He leaned forward.

"That sounds good."

"You'll take it?"

"If I like the alibi."

Craig Armin hitched forward in his chair. "Tonight," he began, "this girl of ours—Letty Burns—is going to Cole Armin with an offer of truce from Monarch. She'll tell Cole Armin and Ted Wallace that you met her on the street and made the proposition. You were afraid to make it to Armin yourself because you knew he would kill you. You want to talk to Armin and Wallace—alone, with none of these women around, in Ted Wallace's rooms. Cole Armin might not want to accept. He's a hothead. But Ted Wallace will make him." He paused. "Do you follow me so far?"

"Sure. She takes the word that I'm comin for a parley and to clear Celia Wallace out."

"That's it. Now do you have five of your bully boys you can trust?"

"More than that," Billings said.

"Good. Put them around that compound behind the Western office. Tell them to shoot Cole Armin on sight if he tries to get out of the house. I don't think he'll try, but we can't take a chance. He'll be up there waiting for you, with the women out of harm's way. You walk up the stairs, knock on the door and when it opens let him have it. If he's waiting in the doorway for you with a gun give the boys the signal to cut down on him. Ted Wallace is in bed. He'll be easy to take care of."

He leaned back. "Afterward you can tell Linton and have your five witnesses to back it up that he started shooting at you when you came in the compound. The men you had brought with you for protection killed Cole Armin in self-defense. The same applies to Ted Wallace. You have me to testify that I sent you to make a truce, and you have Letty Burns to testify that she told Cole Armin that." He spread his hands in a graceful gesture. "What's safer, more airtight than that?"

Billings considered a minute and said, "Nothin', I reckon."

"It suits you?"

Billings nodded. "All except the money."

"What about that?"

"I want it now," Billings said.

Craig Armin leaned back and smiled. "No, Keen. Afterward."

"Now," Billings said.

Craig Armin was a shrewd judge of men, and he saw how stubborn Keen Billings looked. On the other hand, he didn't want Billings jumping town once he had the money.

"Not now," he said quietly and firmly. "Tonight, before you start, you'll have the check—all of it." His voice dropped a little. "And just in case you have any ideas about shoving the blame for this on me if you gum it up, Keen, that check will be made out to 'cash,' not to Keen Billings." He smiled slightly. "I make dozens of checks out that way—so I have no idea who cashes them, you see."

"I see," Keen said, smiling crookedly. "Money's money, just so's I git it."

"Then come up here after dark."

"All right, boss. You can count on me."

He went out, and Craig Armin smiled behind his back. Now that he had made the decision he was glad of it. He felt better.

And when Keen Billings got out into the corridor he leaned against the wall and laughed.

18

Cole was freed at noon. He paid his twenty-five-dollar fine for assaulting a peace officer and received the news that his peace bond was forfeit with a stolid and expressionless face. When Linton led him over from the courthouse back to the sheriff's office and gave him his gun he was troubled by Cole's silence. There was no protest, no sneers, no jibes and no threats—only a complete and indifferent silence.

Linton said, handing him his gun belt, "Don't get me wrong, Armin. We've got nothin' against you in this town so long's you keep in line. I hope you've learned a lesson from this. It cost you quite some money; you should have learned something."

Cole said nothing. He accepted the gun, strapped it on and went out into the street. Linton, his face troubled, followed him for a block. At last, when he saw him turn into the alley behind Western Freight, he concluded that nothing would happen immediately. But he still had his doubts. Armin's eyes were pretty ugly this morning, and he looked as if somebody had lit his fuse.

He was never further from being right. Last night in the dark hours when Cole regained consciousness and realized what had happened he had spent the bitterest moments of his life. This had been the final ignominy. He had one blue chip to spend—the losing of his peace bond in a way that would count, by killing Keen Billings. Instead he had spent it in a barroom scuffle with a deputy sheriff and had been rapped across the skull for his pains.

He didn't falter as he went up the stairs to the rooms. He had reached the final depths of shame last night; all this wouldn't be as bad as confronting his own conscience.

Celia was in the kitchen when he came in. From the bedroom door he could hear Ted's regular breathing, and he guessed he was asleep.

He walked into the kitchen, and Celia turned from the sink. "Hello, Cole," she said quietly.

"Hello, Seely," Cole said, and she looked sharply at him when he said it. He wasn't even aware he had called her that; he had been calling her Seely to himself for a long time now. He sank into a kitchen chair and tilted it against the wall. His long legs sprawled out in front of him. He was unshaven, and there was a fresh cut across his right cheek which overlaid the livid welt of the blacksnake whip.

Celia dried her hands and came over and sat down at the table where she could watch him. "I tried to make them let me see you last night, Cole. They wouldn't. They wouldn't this morning either."

Cole turned his head slowly and smiled at her. "You've been pretty good to me, Celia," he said in a low, bitter voice. "I'm thankful."

Celia laughed shakily. "Cole, that sounds so formal. Almost as if you were saying good-by or something."

"I reckon I meant it to."

Celia hesitated just a moment, and then she said, "You're going then?"

Cole only nodded. His smoky gray eyes were veiled and bitter, and they seemed to pierce Celia's brain and read her very thoughts.

She said, "There's no stopping you. I can see that."

"I come back to explain," Cole said miserably. "I don't want you to think I'm runnin' away, Celia."

Here was a ray of hope, and it blossomed suddenly in Celia's mind. His pride was his vulnerable point. If she accused him of running away maybe he wouldn't go. Desperately she grasped at it and wondered how she could make it sound convincing. She made her first try then.

"It's pretty hard to think anything else, Cole."

Cole looked distressed, and Celia was ashamed of herself, but her face didn't show it.

"No," Cole said slowly. "It ain't that, Celia. I thought it all out last night, layin' there in jail." He looked at his boots now, his smoky eyes musing. His legs were sprawled out in front of him; his hands were in his pockets, and his voice was even, contained. "I never belonged with you and Ted anyway, Seely. I'm a cowman." He smiled crookedly at his boots. "Lord love me, but I'd like to see a cow critter again. I'm sick of lookin' at mules, Seely."

"You're leaving just because you want to see cows again?" Celia taunted.

But Cole was going to have his say. "No, I don't reckon that's it. It's hard to say, Seely." He was still talking to his boots. "A man has got so much in him—so much luck to run out, so many fights to win, so much money to earn, so much liquor to drink and so many friends to make. Usually he's an old man before he works it all out." He shook his head. "But not me. I run my luck out here, Seely. I won every fight except the one with myself. Last night showed it. I let a little runt of a dude sheriff and a couple of his hard-case deputies rawhide me into losing my temper again. The slug I was goin' to spend on Keen Billings never got spent. I wasn't man enough to keep my temper."

"You're pitying yourself," Celia goaded.

Cole looked up at her, his eyes blazing, and then the anger died. He looked back at his boots. "No, you wouldn't understand that. I don't pity myself; I just know what's wrong with me. I'll tell you what it is, too, Seely. I've shot my wad, and it wasn't enough. From now on there's just one thing left for me in this man's town."

"What?"

"Hangin'."

He looked up at Celia to see if she understood that. If she did her face didn't show it. Her mouth twisted up into something close to a sneer.

"Are you afraid, Cole?"

Cole looked at her. In one blinding moment he knew why she was jeering at him. She didn't want him to go! In one wild second he knew that she loved him. He wanted to get up and take her in his arms and tell her what had been in his mind and his heart all these days—and then he relaxed. No, he couldn't do that. Last night, before he even suspected that she loved him, he had made up his mind to do what was best. This didn't change it; it only made it the more bitter. Last night he had known beyond any doubt that he could never help Ted or Celia Wallace again. His last chance to help them by killing Keen Billings had been muffed, and it had cost them five thousand dollars they could not afford. His business was to get out of here. He had tried and failed, and if they were to survive he must walk out. Craig Armin would make some sort of a deal with them so that everything wouldn't be lost. It was he, Cole, that Craig Armin hated, not Ted Wallace.

And then he thought of what Celia had just said. Was he afraid? Maybe it would be easier to leave if he could make her think he was. So he said mildly, "Yes, Seely. That's what I've been tryin' to tell you. I'm afraid."

"I don't believe it!" Celia said sharply, instantly.

Cole didn't smile. He must make this stick if it was the last thing he ever did. It was the least thing he could do for her. He must play the coward, the man who has lost his nerve, and play it convincingly.

He said, "I knew you wouldn't, Seely. You've kind of built me up into a hero, haven't you?" And he looked at her.

Celia was taken aback. It was the truth, but she wasn't going to admit it under these circumstances.

Cole went on, "I got your money for you from Craig Armin. I licked Billings up there on the road. I pulled through with the China Boy wagon." He said bitterly, his voice suddenly harsh, "Can't you understand I did that out of fear, from just bein' plain yellow? When a rat is cornered he'll fight. Juck was goin' to beat me up. I fought, and I got in a lucky swipe that knocked him out. And because Craig Armin knew why I was fightin' he offered to give me the money. And that fight with Billings. I dropped a lighted cigarette on my pony's neck. He reared and pitched me off into Billings. That gunnie shot at me. I crawled against Billings for protection and I bumped his nose, so he couldn't see me. I held to him, to keep from bein' killed, and the gunnie was afraid to shoot. I just bluffed it out."

Celia's mouth was sagging open, and Cole went on relentlessly.

"There's your hero, Celia. Take that brake lever on the wagon breakin'. What would you do with twenty tons of ore behind you and a five-hundred-foot drop on one side of you and a straight-up cliff on the other? You'd run, because you couldn't jump. That's what I done. And I got away with it." He sneered. "There's your hero, Seely. How do you like him?"

Celia came slowly to her feet. There was hurt in her eyes that made Cole's heart ache. "I don't like him," she whispered.

"You still want me to stay?" Cole asked.

"No. No, I—I think you better go."

Celia put her face in her hands and turned her back to Cole. He rose, said, "I'll take the night stage out, Celia. I'll be back to talk with Ted tonight. Then I'll slip out of town tonight quiet-like."

Celia didn't even answer him.

It was ten minutes after Cole was gone, and Celia was sitting at the kitchen table, crying quietly, when she heard the knock at the front door. Quickly she dried her eyes and answered the door. It was Juck and Bill Gurney. Both of them had their hats in their hands, and Juck said, "Cole around, Miss Celia?"

"No. You'll probably find him at the express office, Juck."

Juck frowned and said immediately, "He ain't leavin'?"

"I'm afraid he is, Juck," Celia said in a dead voice. She went back into the house then and left Juck and Bill Gurney standing there.

Slowly Juck tramped down the stairs. At the foot of them he sat down on the bottom step. Bill Gurney, about half his size, sat down beside him, and both of them stared at the fence.

"He hadn't ought to of thought of that," Juck said, "What's Western goin' to do without him?"

"Fold up," Bill Gurney said gloomily.

"What's he doin' it for?" Juck protested.

Bill spat. "What would you do if you was him? That damn sheriff has hog-tied him and strapped him. He's just smart. He's pullin' out before they carry him out."

"But she don't want him to go!" Juck said plaintively. "She's been cryin'!"

Bill Gurney shrugged. "Maybe he don't like her," he suggested. "He can be a right tough hombre in some ways."

"The hell he don't!" Juck said softly. He was quiet a long moment, shifting a wad of tobacco around in his cheek. This was the same thing as quitting, Juck concluded, and that didn't sound like Cole Armin, whatever Bill Gurney said. If Cole was the quitting kind he would have quit long since. No, there was something behind it all. Maybe Cole was just discouraged. A man got like that sometimes. When nothing went right and everybody ganged up on him a man had moments of wanting to quit. Every man did, and Cole wasn't any different than other men. The thing to do was to keep him here until he got over it and was all right again. It was all that simple to Juck, for he was a simple man.

He let loose with a stream of tobacco juice and wiped his mouth with the back of his hand. "We ought to keep him here, Bill."

"How you figure to? Hit him over the head and lock him up somewhere?"

"I ain't hittin' him over the head," Juck answered grimly. "I'd git my jaw broke and you'd git your head unscrewed. No sir, that's out."

"Have him arrested then. That's the next best thing, I reckon."

"He ain't done anything to be arrested for. What could . . ." Juck's voice died, and he stared at the ground. All of a sudden he snapped his fingers loudly. "Well, I'm damned!" he said softly to himself. He stood up. "Come along with me, Bill. I got a idee."

The two of them tramped out of the compound and down the alley to the main street and along it to the sheriff's office.

When Juck, bending his head to get under the lintel, stepped into the sheriff's office there was only a deputy there.

"Where's Linton?" Juck asked.

"I dunno," the deputy said idly.

"Make a guess," Juck said.

The deputy looked irritated. "What do you want of him?"

"I got some questions to ast him. A lot of questions."

"Ask me," the deputy said.

Bill Gurney, who had the average teamster's contempt for the law, snorted. "I'll ask you," he said. "What's two and two? Tomorrow, when you got it figgered out, lemme know. Come on, Juck."

"Wait a minute," Juck said. "Mebbe he'll do. How much law you know, mister?"

"More 'n both you jugheads put together," the deputy said angrily, glaring at Bill Gurney, who glared right back.

"All right," Juck said. "Me 'n Bill was havin' an argument. Bill aims to hold up a stage."

Bill Gurney jerked his head around to look up at Juck. Juck eyed him placidly, and Bill understood that Juck was up to something.

"That's right," Bill said.

The deputy sat up in his chair, glancing from one to the other, alarm stirring in his eyes. "Well, thanks for tellin' me," he said sarcastically. "Want the loan of a gun?"

"I can't tell yet," Bill countered calmly. "Wait'll Juck's through."

Juck went on. "When Bill holds up this stage s'pose there's two people on it—a old man and a old lady. All right, s'pose Bill spends the money he robs from 'em and loses his job. He's got to have another. So he gets a job workin' for the old lady. She knows he's the fella that held her up, but on account of Bill's sweet temper and winnin' ways she don't say nothin' to the sheriff. But the old man knows him too. He goes to the sheriff and tells him. Then Bill is arrested. But the old lady, she won't testify agin' him. She wants to leave town so's she won't have to." Juck paused. "That's what I want to know—can you hold the old lady and lock her up until Bill's trial?"

The deputy just stared at him. "What kind of hammer-headed talk is this?"

"I knowed he couldn't answer us," Bill prodded. "That's why he's a deputy."

"Wait a minute," the deputy said hotly. "I can answer it. Any fool could. Sure, the sheriff could hold her as a material witness."

"How long?" Juck said.

"Until the trial."

"And how long you figure that would be?"

"I dunno. Month, maybe more."

Juck looked at Bill and said seriously, "Well, it don't look like you should ought to work for her, Bill."

The deputy lunged to his feet, the veins standing out on his thick neck. "So you've held up the stage already, Gurney?" he bawled. "You're under arrest!"

"What stage?" Bill asked blankly.

"Why—Juck just said it."

"No. I just *aim* to hold up the stage this old lady rides on," Bill said calmly. "She's comin' in next week some time. Got lots of money, I hear. I was goin' to take the money and then get a job workin' for her." He shook his head. "Don't look like I should ought to now though."

"It don't, for a fact," Juck agreed. "Well, thanks, mister."

"Listen," the deputy said in a thick voice. "I don't know whether you're loco or I am! It's the damnedest thing I ever heard! But if there's a stage held up, Gurney, I'll get a posse out after you and they'll hang you!"

"Much obliged," Bill said, his face serious. "I'll let you know when I do. I aim to take up that offer of the loan of a gun too. Well, so long, mister."

And he and Juck walked out under the bewildered gaze of the angry deputy. The deputy stared at their backs for a long moment, then sat down and scratched his head. He had the conviction that a trick was being played on him, but he couldn't quite tell.

Out on the street Bill said to Juck, "All right, now try and make some sense out of that." He looked at Juck, who was grinning. "What's it all about?"

"You wait and see," Juck said. "Let's go back to the yard."

They turned in the compound, climbed the stairs and again knocked on Celia's door. When she opened it and saw them she said, "Haven't you found him yet, Juck?"

"No ma'am," Juck said, fingering his hat. "I—I'd like to talk to you."

"Come in," Celia said.

"No, this will do," Juck stammered. He tongued his cud of tobacco to the rear of his cheek before he started speaking. "You know, Miss Celia, about me holdin' up the stage that time?"

"Of course. Is there any trouble comin' up?"

"No ma'am." He cleared his throat. "But you see, ma'am, if I was to give myself up Sheriff Linton would want you and Cole for witnesses at my trial."

Celia looked puzzled. "I don't understand, Juck."

"Well, Cole, he can't leave town if the sheriff serves a paper on him as a witness. If he wants to leave town and says he aims to then they can even lock him up till my trial's over. It'll take a month before I'm tried."

And then Celia understood. Juck was willing to go to jail to keep Cole in Piute, by force, if necessary. A swift pity caught at Celia's throat and her eyes misted with tears.

"You'd even go to jail to keep him here, would you, Juck?" Celia asked softly.

"I reckon," Juck agreed quietly. "He don't know what he's doin'. He'll change his mind. Trouble is, when he does he'll be gone."

Celia shook her head. "That's a fine thing to do, Juck. You're a real friend. Only—I doubt if he's worth it."

Juck's gaze whipped up to her. "What?"

"He told me today, Juck, that he was afraid—scared. He wants to leave Piute because he fears for his life."

"He told you that?" Juck said slowly.

Celia nodded. "So I don't think he's worth going to jail for, Juck. I wouldn't give myself up if I were you. I'd let him go."

Juck looked at his hat and then put it on. "Well, good-by, Miss Celia," he said evenly.

He and Bill went downstairs and crossed the compound in silence. At the gate Juck turned and looked back at the door. "Scared," he growled. "Cole Armin told her he was scared."

Bill Gurney's mind worked a little quicker than Juck's, and his intuition was a little keener. He said, "Juck, you and me are buttin' in on somethin' that ain't our business at all. We better keep clear."

"It looks that way," Juck agreed, and then he swore. "But scared? That don't make sense," he said in a hurt and bewildered voice.

19

Letty Burns had just finished drying her few supper dishes when the knock came on her door. She took off her apron, brushed the hair from her eyes, straightened her dress and went to the door.

Keen Billings and Craig Armin stood there on the step.

Craig Armin said, "We'd like to talk with you, Miss Burns."

Here it was, Letty thought dismally. Craig Armin's tone was a command, not a request. She said frantically, "I was going to call on a neighbor, Mr. Armin. What is it?"

"You won't call on your neighbor tonight," Craig Armin said coldly. "May we come in?"

Wordlessly Letty Burns stood aside and let them enter the room, closing the door after them.

Craig Armin put his hat on the table, then gestured toward a chair. "Sit down, Miss Burns. This will take some time."

Silently Letty sank onto the bench, while Armin and Billings, their faces grave, seated themselves.

Craig Armin lighted a cigar, carefully waved out the match, then lifted his cold gaze to hers. "Miss Burns, you've been in Monarch's pay now for some time. And I'm forced to say that you haven't been much help to us."

"I've tried," Letty said quickly.

"Not very hard," Armin corrected. "The other night, by one simple statement, you could have saved me doing what I'm having to do tonight."

Letty sat motionless, waiting for it, holding her breath.

"I'm forced to come to a truce with Western," Craig Armin said.

Letty almost fainted with relief, but she managed to say, "I'm sorry, Mr. Armin. But I suppose it would be best in the end."

"You've been talking to Celia Wallace, I suppose?" Armin said dryly.

"No sir. It just—well, nobody's winning, and you'll both be destroyed."

"So she said," Armin puffed on his cigar. "Well, there's no help for it. We'll make a deal of some kind. I need your help again." He smiled his cold, smug little smile. "You've nothing to fear, my dear. It's all very simple."

"What do you want of me?"

"You know that Cole Armin has threatened to kill both Billings and myself on sight?"

"I heard he was after Mr. Billings."

"And me, too," Armin said. "Naturally I can't send Billings over to Wallace's without some warning or my hotheaded nephew would kill him. You can see that?"

"Why—yes."

"You'll carry the message that Billings is coming then. I want you to go to Wallace's place and tell him that I'm sending Billings over to call a truce and settle this. Armin, since he's a partner, will have to be there too. You must tell them not to attack Billings when he comes. That's simple enough, isn't it?"

"Yes," Letty said with relief.

"Then run along," Armin said. "We'll wait here for you." Letty rose, and Armin said suddenly, "Another thing, Miss Burns. And this is important. I don't want Celia Wallace around the house during the conference. I'll expect you two women to go out calling somewhere until it's over."

Letty didn't know why she thought so, but that was the first false note that had been struck this evening. She said bluntly, "Why?"

Armin was disconcerted. Color crept into his pale face and his eyes shifted away from Letty. Finally he crossed his arms and pulled at the lobe of his right ear with his left hand. Suddenly he rasped out, "Because I said so!"

"Of course," Letty said, surprised at his embarrassment. "I just wondered why."

"You do what you're told and don't ask no questions," Billings said quickly.

"It's all very simple and nothing to get upset about," Armin said smoothly. "I happen to know, because I've been told, that Celia Wallace hates me. Twice she's tried to talk me into a truce, and twice I've refused her. If she's with Ted Wallace tonight she'll tell him to hold out for a better offer. I don't want her around because —well, naturally, I want the best of this deal if Billings can get it."

"I see," Letty said. But she didn't. Craig Armin was watching her closely.

"So I want it understood," Armin went on firmly, "that you'll take her away from there, Miss Burns."

"I'll do it," Letty said. She went over to the wardrobe, opened it and got out her hat. Then she reached up on the top shelf for her pocketbook. As she lifted it down the flap opened and her gun clattered to the floor.

Billings lunged for it, going to his knees, and when he got it he came to his feet, his face ugly.

"What are you tryin' to pull?" he asked thickly.

Letty was surprised at the vehemence of his question. "Why, I always carry it," she said. "I'm a single woman, Mr. Billings, and this town is pretty rough. I carry it in case I'm molested."

Billings was still eying her suspiciously. "Well, you won't carry it tonight," he said. He turned and tossed the small gun into the chair where he had been sitting. It landed on the pillow, clattered against the back, then slid down, half hidden by the pillow.

"Get goin'," Billings said harshly.

Meekly and swiftly Letty finished her business.

It was strange how jumpy and nervous they were, Letty thought. There was nothing to be nervous about in what they were planning. And they didn't even trust her. She touched her small hat, turned away from the mirror and faced Craig Armin, who was standing.

"How soon will Mr. Billings be along?" Letty asked.

"Ten minutes after you, my dear," Armin said. "Just so you tell them he's on his way and clear Celia Wallace out. I'll wait here, if I may."

"Certainly," Letty said. She went to the door, said good-by and stepped out into the night. Slowly she walked up toward the dark street, and the further she went the slower became her pace. This was all so very queer, their actions so suspicious. They didn't seem like two men who were relieved that at last their long fight was going to be settled. And she stopped in the darkness of the yard and half turned to look back at her lamplit window. They hadn't saved her for this—an errand any little boy could do for a quarter.

Her mind made up, she went softly back to the door and put her ear against it. She could hear a rumble of voices but no words. Still not satisfied, she moved over to the window and looked in. Craig Armin was standing up, writing something at the table. They had found her pen and ink and were using it. Then Armin straightened up and handed what he had been writing to Keen Billings. It was a check. Billings nodded approvingly, put the check in his vest pocket and sat down.

Letty faded away into the night and hurried on her way. Why would Armin be giving Keen Billings a check now? She didn't know, but she had a premonition. It was unreasonable and illogical, but it was there, nevertheless. The whole thing didn't seem right, and she felt a cold and sudden fear.

A few minutes later, when she walked into the empty compound behind Western's office, Letty had come to a momentous decision. And now that she had she could scarcely contain herself.

She raced up the steps, knocked on the door and waited impatiently.

Celia answered the door, saw who it was and opened it wide. "Come in, Letty."

"Celia, is Cole here?"

"Yes. He's in with Ted. Why?"

Letty didn't answer. She hurried around the table and into the corridor and then into Ted's room. Cole was hunkered down against the wall by the window. Both he and Ted looked at her and saw the alarm on her face.

Ted pulled himself up in bed as Celia came in behind Letty, and he said, "Letty, what's happened?"

"I haven't got much time to tell you!" Letty said swiftly. "Craig Armin and Keen Billings came over to my house! They told me to come over here and tell you that Keen Billings was coming over in ten minutes to talk with you. Monarch wants to come to a truce!"

Ted looked at Cole and grinned. "There you are, boy! Hear that?"

"No, no, Ted!" Letty cried. "I don't think they mean it!"

"Why don't you?" Cole drawled quietly.

"They're nervous, both of them. And more than that, they told me to get Celia out of the house before Keen Billings came!"

"Why?" Ted asked.

"Oh, does it matter?" Letty cried. "I know there's something behind it! I don't know what they're planning, but it didn't ring true, Ted!"

Cole came to his feet. Ted was looking at him and so was Celia, but Cole's smoky eyes were on Letty.

"Is this another trick, Letty?" Cole asked quietly.

"Trick?" Ted asked.

Cole spoke to Ted, but he was watching Letty. "I can't prove it, Ted," he said quietly, "but I think Letty is workin' for Monarch."

Ted said furiously, "You're a liar!"

Letty's face went pale then.

Cole went on stubbornly, "It's no business of mine, Ted. I'm out of this. But it's my hunch. And I think she's tryin' to trick us again."

"Damn you!" Ted shouted. "You can't say that about her!"

Letty said harshly, "Wait!" They all looked at her. "It's true! Cole's right. I *am* being paid by Keen Billings and Craig Armin! Oh, they told me that Ted was the one who killed Pete, my brother." She looked at Ted. "Maybe you did, Ted. Only I can't hate you for it, can't see these terrible things happen to you any longer! I'm telling the truth now!"

"But I didn't kill your brother, Letty!" Ted cried. "I never killed a man in my life! I didn't even know him!"

Letty looked searchingly at him. "He was a Monarch teamster," Letty said slowly. "You didn't loosen the kingbolt on his wagon that time? He broke——"

"I know he broke his legs and died of gangrene," Ted said fiercely. "But I didn't do it, Letty. I'll swear by all that's holy that I'd kill a man who did that!"

"But Billings said you did!"

"He lies, damn him!"

Letty shook her head and buried her face in her hands for a moment. She wasn't going to cry. She couldn't cry now when all of them depended on her.

"Then you must listen to me now!" she said swiftly. "Something awful is going to happen, I know!"

Cole said coldly, "You lied once, Letty. You tried to sell us out. How do we know you aren't doin' it again?"

"You've got to believe me!" Letty cried.

"Cole, she's telling the truth," Celia said.

"Maybe," Cole said tonelessly, watching Letty. "Now tell it again. Tell the truth, Letty. What did they say?"

"They said for me to go over and tell both of you that they wanted to come to terms. You'd threatened to kill Billings when you saw him again, and they were afraid you'd shoot him when he came if I didn't warn you."

"Billings?" Cole echoed. "Why doesn't Craig Armin come?"

"I don't know. He's waiting at my place!" Letty wailed. "I'm just telling you."

"Go on."

"Then Craig Armin said I was to get Celia out of the house and go somewhere with her."

"Why did he say that?" Cole insisted.

"That's what I wondered! I asked him why. He got embarrassed then. His face got red and he pulled his ear, like an embarrassed man will. He told me that——"

She stopped talking. A change had come over Cole Armin's face. A look of utter, blank astonishment. Celia and Ted looked at him. Cole's face was drawn, tense.

Slowly he walked over to Letty, put both hands on her shoulders and shook her. "Letty, what did you say just then?" he asked in a thick voice.

"When?"

"What did Craig Armin do when you asked him why?"

"He got red. The color came——"

"I don't mean that!" Cole said savagely. "What else?"

"He—he pulled his ear—the lobe of his ear, like a man does when he's embarrassed."

"Are you sure?"

"Why—yes," Letty faltered. "I think I'm right. Why?"

"Which ear?" Cole's hands were squeezing Letty's shoulders until she winced.

Letty thought. "His right ear, I think."

"Are you sure it was his right ear?" Cole demanded and shook her again. "Are you sure?"

"I am," Celia put in swiftly. "I've seen him do it, Cole. I've talked with him twice, pled with him twice, and each time I've accused him of wanting this murder. And each time he's been embarrassed. And each time when he gets like that he pulls his ear."

"His right ear?" Cole demanded.

Celia nodded. "I'm sure it's his right ear. He's left-handed and he crosses his arms." She stopped talking. "Why, Cole?"

Cole's hands slipped from Letty's shoulders. He looked at them blankly, his lips barely moving.

And then he said, "Because my uncle, Craig Armin, lost half of his right ear in the Mexican War! It was shot away! I remember my dad tellin' me!"

He looked steadily at Celia.

"This man is not Craig Armin," he said slowly.

20

For a moment they looked at him, too stunned to speak. Then Cole spoke sharply to Letty: "How long did they say, Letty, before Billings would come?"

"Ten minutes."

"And he was comin' alone?"

"Craig Armin said so."

Cole looked at Ted. "Not alone. He'll have men with him. And we're trapped here, Ted, like they want us! That's why they wanted the women out—so they could shoot me and then come in and get you!"

"That's right!" Letty cried. "That must be it!"

Cole looked around the room. "Celia, you and Letty get out of here! Quick!"

"But what about Ted?" Celia asked.

"I'm goin' to carry him over to the new yard and fort up in a wagon over there!" He said swiftly to Ted, "You got a gun?"

Ted pulled it out from under the blankets.

Cole said, "Go on, Celia! You and Letty go!" To Ted he said, "I'll try and make it easy, fella, but it will hurt!"

"Go ahead," Ted said quietly.

Celia and Letty went into the other room. Cole picked Ted up, blankets and all, slung him over his shoulder, pulled his gun and went out into the corridor.

Celia was standing in the doorway, looking over her shoulder at Cole.

"Get on!" Cole said.

"I'll get help, Cole," Celia said.

"You hide!" Cole said miserably. "Don't show your head. Hide in the office!"

But Celia was gone down the steps.

Cole rounded the table and said to Ted, "I'll take it easy, boy," and went out the door.

As soon as he hit the platform a crash of gunfire broke out. The slugs rapped in the wood of the doorframe, and Cole counted four different reports. A window, somewhere in the other rooms, crashed in, and a man yelled, "They're out in back. Get the steps!"

Swiftly, then, Cole made his decision. To go back would invite death, because Billings' men had come in on the roof of the adjoining building. Safety lay down there and in the new wagon yard. Celia and Letty were already in the office below.

He palmed up his gun and shot once, and the lantern on the gate went out. Then he lunged down the steps, the sound racketing out into the night.

Five rifles now opened up at him. He could hear the slugs slapping into the wood of the building in front of him and behind him.

He hit the ground below, staggered, fell to his knees, caught himself and came erect.

Ted, slung over his shoulder, opened up now at the two riflemen along the side fence of the compound.

Cole clung to the nearest side fence and ran. A gun went off almost in his face, but he did not change his stride. Ted raised his gun and shot, and a man screamed, and then the other two riflemen, beaten to cover by Ted's fire, opened up again. And Ted couldn't shoot, for his gun was empty.

They were nearing the alley now, the shots raking the darkness and slapping into the board fence.

And then they were almost at the gate, when a man loomed up there in the middle of it, his body framed by the dim light in the wagon yard across the way. The man raised a rifle, and Cole frantically whipped up his gun, running still. He shot and the man bent over, and Cole slashed out with his gun as he reached him. The man sprawled backward into the alley, and now it was clear.

As he was crossing the alley someone from far down the alley cut loose with a shot that geysered up the dust ahead of him.

That would be Billings. Cole couldn't shoot now, for his gun was empty too. He heard Ted say softly, "Run for it, boy."

There was one big ore wagon back against the corner of the stable and the rear fence, and Cole could barely make it out in the lantern light. But he ran for it, knowing that it would take these men a few seconds to leg up over the compound fence and follow him.

His legs were giving out, for Ted was heavy, and the sweat was pouring off his forehead. His back crawled, and he was waiting for the first shot that would catch him in the back and knock him flat on his face.

And then he heard Ted shoot. Ted, hanging over his back, had fumbled out some shells from Cole's belt and reloaded, and now he shot at the first man who charged through the gate. The wagon was only yards away now, and Cole drove his buckling knees to make it. He reached the wagon just as two riflemen opened up on them from the compound gate.

Mercifully the tail gate of the wagon was down. Cole rolled Ted off his shoulder into the wagon bed and then dived in alongside him, just as the whole chorus of rifle fire opened in concert and the heavy plank sides of the wagon drummed with the slugs.

"All right?" he asked Ted, panting.

"Not hit," Ted said through clenched teeth. "Here's my gun. Gimme yours and I'll load."

Cole poked his head out of the rear of the ore wagon and saw a man streaking for a bale of hay that lay on the ground by the trough. He shot and the man dived behind the hay. But while he was trying three more men had sought shelter in the wagon yard, forting up behind the trough, another ore wagon and the corner of the stable.

And then Keen Billings' voice, hoarse with wrath, yelled, "Rush him, boys!"

Cole emptied his gun in the direction of the voice and he heard Billings laugh. While he traded guns with Ted he saw the men move closer. They were like Indians, drifting from cover to cover until they were close enough to attack.

Ted said grimly, "We're in a spot, Cole."

"I can't see a damn thing!" Cole raged. "I'm goin' to stand up. But when they shoot that light out they'll rush. Be ready for it."

Ted said quietly, "Cole, in case you pull out of this and I don't you'll watch out for Celia."

"If you go I go," Cole said simply.

"No. I want you to clear out. On her account."

"Nothin' doin'," Cole said. "I'm not clearin' out."

"Please, for——"

"No!" Cole said harshly. "I got us into most of this, Ted. I'm sellin' out the hard way!"

He rose then and saw a man drifting in to the cover of the stable door. He snapped a shot at him, but the man didn't duck. It was Billings. Very carefully Billings took sight at the lantern hanging on a nail down the stable and shot it out.

There was utter blackness then, and Cole felt cold despair grip him. They were trapped now, trapped for fair. He couldn't leave Ted, and Keen Billings knew he wouldn't.

Keen's voice lifted again in a bawl. "The lantern's out, boys. Rush him."

Cole shot blindly at anything that moved, but he could not be certain of any sight in that pitch dark. When a shot bloomed orange he shot at it, but each time the shots were getting closer. And back where it was safe, at the head of the stable, Keen Billings was yelling: "Get 'em, boys. A hundred dollars a scalp!"

Ted shot then and close by the end of the wagon Cole heard a man curse. And then the others opened up. They were a tight little half circle now, only yards away, and they were running.

Cole fanned his gun empty, and as the hammer clicked on the last empty he heard a great bawling voice call:

"Hold 'em, Cole! Here we come!"

It was Juck. He and other men were pouring out of the back door of the office across the alley.

Cole yelled: "Come on, Juck," and Ted opened up with the last of his load.

Frantically Cole reloaded. For one second there were no shots from Billings' men. And in that silence, up at the front of the yard, they could hear the heavy steps of a man running toward the gate.

It was Billings. And his men heard it too.

One man called, "He's runnin'. Let's light a shuck."

Cole ran to the front of the wagon, climbed it and leaped to the stable roof. He went over it, dropped on the other side into the new yard and then ran blindly diagonally across it, leaping piles of lumber and dodging what he couldn't leap. Ted was safe, he knew. And Billings would make the gate long before Juck would get out of the compound. Once he was out of the gate what would Billings do? He'd run down the alley away from town.

And Cole staked everything on that guess.

He approached the alley fence far down toward the side street, and he heard Billings pounding down the alley on the other side. Cole leaped for the fence, hauled himself up, then dropped into the alley.

Billings, his back to him, was almost at the street, his body silhouetted against the faint lights of the town.

Cole dropped to the ground, rolled to his knees and then called sharply, "Billings!"

Billings hauled up, then turned slowly around.

"Make your play, Keen. This is it!" Cole's voice was mild, but it had the ring of iron in it.

Keen peered into the dark alley. He could make out Cole's form as Cole came to his knees. He had an impulse to surrender, and then in one blinding flash he knew that he couldn't. And he knew that he might be able to catch Cole off balance and winded if he acted now.

His hand slapped down at his gun, wrapped around the butt and hauled it out.

Cole saw it come, just as his cleared leather. Keen shot hurriedly then from the hip. Shot twice. And Cole swung the black shape of Keen in his sights, and when his gun sight blacked out he pulled the trigger. He shot three times, and at the third shot Keen slacked below the sight and fell on his back.

Slowly Cole lowered his gun and walked over to him and stood above him, looking down. His two shots had caught Keen in the face.

Behind him he could hear the ruckus in the alley, the shouting and the talk and excitement. But he only listened to it absently.

Hadn't Letty said that Craig Armin was waiting at her house? She had. He headed for the street then and Letty's house, his gun still in his hand, and when Girard caught up with him as he rounded the corner of the alley Cole didn't look at him.

"Stay out of my way," Cole warned the man at his side.

21

Craig had heard the prolonged gunfire. To him it meant only one thing: that Cole Armin and Wallace were dead and Monarch was supreme in Piute. He smiled with pleasure at the thought, pleased with his plan and certain of its outcome. Presently someone would be here to tell him about it, and he must have his face composed. He was planning just how to assume the right expression of regret for the sudden death of a bitter and hated rival when he heard the footsteps outside.

He went to the door, thinking maybe it was Keen Billings already, and he opened it.

Cole Armin shoved the door open and stepped into the room. There was a man behind him, but Craig Armin never saw that man.

He backed away from Cole Armin as if he had seen the dead, and before he could get his wits together Cole Armin said slowly, "It didn't work, Craig. They missed me."

Craig tried to speak and couldn't. Girard came over to him, slapped his pockets to see whether he carried a gun or not, then stepped back.

Cole said, "Sit down!"

Girard shoved him backward into the nearest chair. Then Cole stalked over to him and stood above him. "Before I kill you, Armin, just tell me who you are. You're not Craig Armin."

Armin couldn't talk yet. Cole leaned over and cuffed him sharply across the face. Cole's face was white as chalk, and there was murder in his eyes.

"I—I'm Craig Armin," Armin said weakly.

Cole reached over, grabbed Armin's lapels and hauled him out of his seat. He said wickedly, "You lie! Damn your black soul! You lie! Now talk!" And he threw him back into the chair with such violence that the chair creaked.

When Craig Armin hit the chair seat he sat on something hard as rock, and the pain of it jarred him. And then through his fright he remembered. He had sat on Letty Burns's gun that Billings had taken away from her.

Slowly he put his hand around behind him, and the gun slipped into his fingers. Neither Cole Armin nor Girard had a gun out.

Craig Armin lunged to his feet, whipping the gun out in front of him and kicking back at the chair at the same time.

There was a smile of cruel elation on his face as he said, "What did you ask me?"

Girard, dismay in his face, shoved his hands to the ceiling. Cole looked at the gun, and he remembered it. He also remembered what was in it. Slowly, then, he put up his hands and stepped back.

"I come damn close," he said quietly.

"But not close enough," Craig Armin said. "It won't be terribly hard to explain to Linton why I had to kill you."

Cole licked his lips and looked at Girard. Girard was facing it with a stolid look of distaste.

"You're goin' to—to shoot us?" Cole asked.

"I have to. You've forced me," Craig answered.

Cole didn't speak for a moment. This was Craig Armin's minute of triumph, and he was making the best of it. With cruel and sadistic delight he was enjoying this.

Cole said in a voice without hope, "I'm not beggin' you for anything, Armin. When a man's time comes it comes. But I'd like to ask some questions before you let that thing off in my face."

"If that's a stall, Armin, it won't work," Craig Armin said coldly. "The first person I hear outside I'll shoot you."

"Then I can talk?"

"As long as I want you to. Go ahead."

Cole looked at the gun and then at Craig Armin, "You're not Craig Armin."

"No. How did you know?"

"I didn't until tonight. I never saw my uncle. But tonight I remembered somethin'. Letty and Celia said when you get cornered you pull your ear—your right ear lobe."

"I may have. I don't remember."

"My dad told me that my uncle Craig had the lobe of his right ear shot off in the Mexican War. It took me a hell of a while to remember it."

"That's right. The real Craig Armin did have part of his ear missing. I didn't think you'd notice it since you never saw him."

"And where is he?"

Craig Armin smiled. "In a jail in Missouri, where I put him. I framed him for murder. And because I looked like him I took his name so I could get his money out of a St. Louis bank." He smiled wolfishly. "I've built it into quite a little stake."

"Is he alive?"

"He's alive, and he'll be on my trail in another three months," Craig Armin said slowly. "That's why I got you out here."

Cole scowled and said, "I don't get it."

"I'll have to talk fast," Craig Armin said quickly, still smiling. "I knew the real Craig Armin would track me down when he got out of jail. He'd told me about you, so I wrote you to come here. I planned to leave this business to you and go to the Coast. With you here, believing I was your uncle, you'd send me half the money from the Monarch. When the real Craig Armin arrived you'd arrest him as an imposter, and I'd still get my money. But if he convinced you I was a fraud I had time to get away. It was clever, wasn't it? Only you proved to be a little too chivalrous. You fought with me and made me return the money to the Wallaces. I even counted on you fighting them to a standstill." He shrugged. "It didn't work. You've put me to considerable trouble. But I've won, you see. I always win."

Cole said, "It's cagey, all right. Have I got any more time?"

"A little. I don't hear anyone coming."

"Who set fire to the Monarch?"

Craig Armin laughed then. "I did."

Cole stared at him. "Your own outfit?"

"That's right. You see, I wanted you in jail, out of the way. First, when Billings hired Letty Burns, we counted on her to tell us how to ruin you. The first chance we got was when we put you onto Jim Rough. But Billings is timid. After that beating he didn't want to touch the wagon. He was afraid of what you'd do. I sawed the brake lever myself. I hoped, if the accident didn't kill you, you'd kill Billings." He shook his head. "Billings, you see, had too much on me. I hoped you'd kill him and Linton would jail you. You didn't kill him. Then I hoped, by setting the fire and putting the blame on you, that Linton would jail you for that. Letty Burns ruined that."

"So you were tryin' to put Billings out of the way and me out of the way too?"

"Exactly. Clever, but it didn't work." He paused. "Your time is up, I think."

"One more question," Cole said calmly. "Who shoved Ted Wallace down the stairs?"

Craig bowed mockingly. "I did. I hoped it would kill you both."

Girard said hoarsely, "Get it over with!"

"Wait!" Cole said swiftly. "You shoved Ted; you sawed the brake lever and you burned the Monarch. Did you blow up the China Boy?"

This time Craig Armin bowed in Girard's direction, the gun trained on Cole. "I did. I figured surely that you would kill Billings then for spoiling your contract. And I was just as sure Linton would arrest you and hang you for the killing. That didn't work either, so I was driven to this." He glanced at Cole. "Partly by your shot at me last night. It stampeded me to a decision."

Cole ignored that and said slowly, "And now you'll do what, Armin?"

"When I get this explained," Armin said, "I'm putting the Monarch and its freighting contracts up for sale. I should realize a nice tidy sum. Then I'll be well out of the country before the real Craig Armin gets here." His face changed, and he stopped talking. There was the faint sound of someone running. "Time's up," he said crisply. "I'll get you out of the way first, Cole. Back up, Girard!"

Girard backed up, his face bathed in sweat.

When Craig Armin looked at Cole, Cole was smiling faintly.

"It's funny?" he asked icily.

Cole didn't answer. He said, "I'm comin' for you, Armin. I'm comin' slow."

And he started to walk. Craig Armin's face set and he pulled the trigger. There was an explosion, but Cole was still walking afterward.

"Thanks for confessin', and in front of a witness," Cole murmured.

Craig Armin stepped backward in panic and shot again. And Cole still walked toward him.

Then Craig Armin took a step forward, placed the gun two feet from Cole and emptied it into him.

Cole laughed then. "They're blanks."

And he knocked Craig Armin over the table with a smashing blow in the face.

At that moment Celia ran into the open doorway. Cole didn't see her. Girard reached over, took Celia by the arm, hauled her against the wall and said, "Quiet, girl. Can you watch it?"

Celia nodded mutely.

Cole put the lamp on the cabinet behind him, then turned the table over against the wall. Craig Armin was backed against the stove now. His face was a green color, and all his false courage had left him.

He fumbled around the stove and found the poker, just as Cole came at him. He raised it high over his head, his face twisted with rage, just as Cole's big fist smashed into his face again. He caromed into the stove, overturned it and landed in a heap in the corner. Cole pounced on him, pulled him up, kicking and fighting, and again he smashed him in the face. Craig Armin sprawled clear across the room and was brought up against the far wall with a crash. The iron-framed mirror crashed to the floor at his feet and the glass broke.

His mouth runneling blood, Craig Armin staggered to his feet, brandishing the mirror frame.

Celia gasped and said, "Cole, watch out!"

But Cole was deaf. He came at Craig Armin, and Armin swung the frame savagely. Cole half broke the force of the blow with his elbow and then he tackled Armin and they went down.

They rolled over and over on the floor, and when they came to a stop, Cole on the bottom, Craig Armin had his hands around Cole's throat.

Cole pulled them away as if they were straw, and then he gripped Armin by the throat and rolled over on top of him.

He straddled him then and choked him. Cole's lips were drawn over his teeth and his eyes were hot.

Craig Armin thrashed around on the floor and tore at Cole's big hands, and his face turned red and then purple.

Celia moaned, "Stop him!"

She and Girard lunged for Cole and tried to pull him off. Just then Linton burst into the room, three townspeople and Letty Burns and Juck behind him, along with a half-dozen teamsters.

Linton rapped out, "Pull him off."

Juck said, "Leave him be!"

Celia turned and cried, "Juck, help me!"

Juck softened then. He and Linton and Girard and another man tried to pull Cole off. But Cole was crazy with rage.

As they pulled Cole to his feet Craig Armin, locked in those big hands, came too. They fought Cole and tried to break his hold. And they couldn't. Cole suddenly dropped Craig Armin and then stood there, breathing hard, his arms held by the other men.

Linton bent down over Craig Armin and felt his pulse. Then he picked up a shard of the mirror and held it to Craig Armin's black lips.

Turning, afterward, he looked at Cole. "Well, you've killed him, my boy. Plain, damned murder!"

22

"Murder, hell!" Girard roared. "He tried to kill us!"

"Nevertheless, it's murder," Linton said calmly. He stroked his mustache and looked at Cole, who was still breathing deeply, his eyes wild and uncontrolled.

"Careful, Sheriff," Cole warned. "Be damned careful."

"That man wasn't even Craig Armin," Girard said. He pushed his way through the crowd to Linton. And there, while Cole looked on, Girard told the story of Armin disclosing his real identity. As he talked Linton, who had watched the fight at the compound and had even taken shots at Cole and Ted Wallace, knew that his scheme had met with abysmal failure. Western had won out, and Billings and Craig Armin were dead. And like the true politician he was Linton knew that he had to get on the winning side and do it fast. The best way was by pretending ignorance.

At the finish of Girard's speech he said, "Well, that's different. A man has a right to kill in self-defense." He looked up at the crowd. "Anyone see this ruckus at the compound?"

"I did," Juck said.

"What happened?"

Juck told him what he had seen. Celia put in what she had seen. When they were finished Linton said, "And where's Billings?"

"He's dead," a teamster said.

"Dead, eh?" Linton said. "Both of them dead—Armin and Billings?"

Letty Burns spoke up quietly. "Didn't you see it, Sheriff?"

"Why, no," Sheriff Linton said easily. "I came up the street and somebody told me Craig Armin and Cole were having it out. I ran for the house here."

"You didn't know Billings was dead?" Letty insisted.

"Not till about ten seconds ago," Linton said easily.

Letty strode out to face him, eyes flashing. Suddenly she reached in the top pocket of his vest and pulled out a piece of paper. "How do you explain that check?" Letty said.

Linton, who had already looked at it, said, "Armin gave me that check this morning."

"You lie," Letty said. "I was standing in the shadow of those buildings when you took it from Keen Billings' pocket."

"You're lyin'!" Linton said hotly.

Letty wheeled to face Cole. "Maybe this will prove I'm not a traitor, Mr. Armin! I saw Sheriff Linton take that from Billings' pocket! I saw Billings put it there earlier in the evening." She pointed an accusing finger at Linton. "How did he know to look in Billings' pocket for the check if he didn't know Billings would have it? Answer me that!"

Cole said slowly, "That money was paid to Billings for gulchin' Ted and me, Linton. How come you knew he'd have it?"

"I forgot," Linton said weakly. "I did see Billings. I searched him. Part of my job, you know."

"Then why did you say you didn't?" Cole insisted.

"I—well, I don't know."

Celia said coldly, "You mean you didn't want to be associated with Billings, Mr. Linton?"

Linton wheeled to face her. "Why shouldn't I want to be? I tell you I forgot!"

Celia's voice was sharp with scorn. "I'll tell you why you didn't want to be associated with Billings. You were there and watched him try to kill Ted and Cole! You stood there and let them do it!"

"You lie!" Linton shouted.

Celia said swiftly, "You admit you took the check?"

"Yes."

"Then you're the man," Celia said. "Because I followed a man out of the wagon yard and down the alley, because I was hunting for Cole. And I saw this man take a paper from Billings' pocket. If you admit one you admit that you watched Billings try and kill them."

There was a long silence, and Juck suddenly said, "Any rope around here?"

"No! No!" Linton cried. "You're lyin'. You're framing me!"

Cole walked up to him and grabbed him by the coat and twisted him to his knees.

"Juck, get that rope," Cole said. "This man can't tell the difference between hangin' and talkin' and goin' free."

"Wh-what?" Linton asked.

"I said, you're goin' to hang if you keep your mouth shut. There's no law here to stop us, because we'll lynch you and you're the law. But if you talk you'll only get run out of town. You didn't kill anybody, did you?"

"Lynch him anyway!" Juck growled.

"I'll talk!" Linton cried. "I want your promise first."

Cole held out his hand. "Give me a gun."

Somebody slipped him a gun. "The first man that makes a move toward Linton gets shot," he announced. "Get up and talk!"

Linton scrambled to his feet. "Billings and me were in it together," he panted. "We figured to whittle down both the Western and Monarch until Craig Armin paid Billings to kill you and Ted Wallace! Last night Billings shot at Craig Armin, and that swung it. He told Keen to kill you. We planned, after you was dead, to blackmail Armin, to throw him out of Monarch and take it over. With you and Wallace dead, and not many freightin' companies, we figured to get all the contracts for Monarch. And I could hush it up, being sheriff." He looked wildly at Cole. "Are you goin' to free me?"

Cole shoved him toward the door. Then he lifted his booted foot and kicked Linton savagely out the door. They heard him scramble to his feet and run as fast as he could through the night.

Juck said, "I aim to make sure he gets out," and headed for the door.

"Remember what I said, Juck," Cole called.

"I ain't goin' to hurt him," Juck growled, and then he grinned. "I'm just goin' to make almighty sure he leaves town."

The other teamsters and townspeople followed Juck out. There were only Girard and Letty and Celia left, besides Cole.

Cole said gently, "Letty, I take back everything I said about you."

Letty smiled. "You were right, Cole." She put out her hand. "Terribly right—except when you thought I'd sell you out the last time." She looked at Celia. "I have such a lot to make up to you."

"Try making it up to Ted," Celia said in a kindly voice. "I'm sure Mr. Girard will take you back to him, Letty."

Girard and Letty went out into the night. Celia looked over at Cole, who was watching her.

"Let's get out of here, Seely," Cole said. He turned her away from the sight of Craig Armin dead on the floor.

They stepped out into the night and went out to the road. Celia said suddenly, "Cole, no man ever told as big a lie as you did when you said you were leaving town because you were afraid. I know that now. Why did you do it?"

Cole stopped and Celia did too. He put his hands on her shoulders and turned her to face him. "I had to, Seely. Haven't you guessed why?"

"No, Cole. I've tried and I can't."

"It was on account of somethin' I saw in your eyes."

"In my eyes? What?"

Cole hesitated only a moment, then he said quietly, "If I'm wrong, Seely, I'm sorry. You really want me to tell you?"

"I asked, didn't I?" Celia said in a soft voice.

Cole said gently, "You were rawhidin' me last night, Celia, because you didn't want me to go. Did you?"

"No, I didn't," Celia confessed.

"That's what I saw in your eyes," Cole murmured. "And I had

to say I was scared, because I was sinkin' you and Ted, Seely. I—
I . . ." His voice died away.

"You what, Cole?"

"I loved you so much I couldn't drag you down with me, I
reckon."

"Oh, Cole," Celia said softly. "And I loved you so much that I
didn't want to live if you weren't near me!"

"That's really what I saw in your eyes," Cole said.

"Of course you did!" Celia cried. "Are you blind, dear?"

"Only as blind as you, I reckon," Cole said. "Because I've
looked the same way a mighty long time."

"Too long," Celia said. "Way too long, Cole."

And Cole kissed her then, because they had talked too much
already, and he found that Celia thought so too.